Zane's chest swelled with admiration for the strong young woman. Add "new mom" to her task list. He hoped he wasn't making a mistake in offering his help, but somehow her vulnerability had penetrated his better judgment. That much he recognized.

She was John's sister. Chad, John's son. Zane owed it to his friend and partner to help his sister make this work. If he discovered what he needed to know in the process, so much the better. He noticed her staring at him and became aware he'd been caught up in his thoughts. He stood.

She folded her arms across her chest and raised her eyebrows. "You know, you never did tell me why you dropped by. I know it wasn't for pleasantries, since you've already stated at the funeral and on the phone that you needed to speak to me. It was important. Remember?"

"I have a proposition for you."

ELIZABETH GODDARD is a seventh-generation Texan transplanted in Southern Oregon near the Rogue River. She loves to write and read inspirational fiction in several genres, including thriller, suspense, historical, and speculative fiction. When she's not writing, she's busy homeschooling her four children and serving with her husband as he pastors a local church. She enjoys hiking in the Redwoods and camping on the Oregon coast with her family. Find out more about Beth at www.elizabethgoddard.com.

Seasons
of Love

Elizabeth Goddard

Heartsong Presents

Dedicated to my loving husband, Dan; my four beautiful children, Rachel, Christopher, Jonathan, and Andrew; and my ever-supportive parents. Special thanks to Chief Arthur Parker of the Carver, Massachusetts, police department; Flax Pond Farms; Centennial Cranberry Farms; and Brian Kendig for helping me to understand encryption software.

A note from the Author:
I love to hear from my readers! You may correspond with me by writing:

Elizabeth Goddard
Author Relations
PO Box 721
Uhrichsville, OH 44683

ISBN 978-1-59789-899-7

SEASONS OF LOVE

Scripture quotations are taken from the HOLY BIBLE, NEW INTERNATIONAL VERSION®. NIV®. Copyright © 1973, 1978, 1984 by International Bible Society. Used by permission of Zondervan. All rights reserved.

All of the characters and events in this book are fictitious. Any resemblance to actual persons, living or dead, or to actual events is purely coincidental.

Our mission is to publish and distribute inspirational products offering exceptional value and biblical encouragement to the masses.

PRINTED IN THE U.S.A.

prologue

"I've got a proposition for you. Call me," a familiar voice crackled from the answering machine.

Grandpa? Riley O'Hare set her sack of groceries on the counter as she replayed the message.

The clock on the sage-colored wall displayed six thirty. Grandpa was on the East Coast. No way would he still be up at nine thirty. She'd have to wait until morning before she could call him. She hated waiting and stared at the ceiling while the annoying computerized voice detailed the time and stated that she had another message.

"Riley, it's Eric. You there? I tried to reach you on your cell today. I'd love to have dinner with you tonight, but I've got that meeting with Tom Carling at Solution Sciences, remember? Actually, you could join me. It never hurts to have a beautiful woman on your arm. Italiano's at six thirty."

"Too late," she said and huffed at his comment. It irritated her that he acted as though they were supposed to have dinner tonight. When would he get it? He didn't seem to understand that things were over between them. Riley shuddered.

Eric Rutherford only saw her as eye candy to impress his colleagues. Everything revolved around his work as a business consultant—though she couldn't blame him for that. Her career as a regional account executive for Morris & Associates consumed her, as well. Most people didn't have time to live their own lives anymore.

Anxious to be rid of thoughts of Eric, she hit the DELETE button hard and long. The answering machine responded that all messages had been erased.

"What? Argh." Riley examined the caller ID list to see whose calls she'd missed since she'd just accidentally trashed all the messages. John's work number appeared last. She called her brother back, getting no answer; then she tried his cell. Still no answer, so she left a message.

After she finished putting away the groceries she'd grabbed on the way home from work, she popped precooked chicken strips onto a paper plate and into the microwave, then pulled the tab off a diet soda. It fizzed over the top and onto her beige blouse. "Ack!" She whirled around and held it over the sink. When the soda's overzealous carbonation died down, she wiped the can with a paper towel and set it on the counter while she cleaned.

Frustration overwhelmed her. She didn't have the energy to cook a decent meal. Life had been hectic since graduating from college with a business degree. Three years of her life had flown by since then. Was this what it was all about?

Riley sat at the kitchen counter and ate her chicken strips, her thoughts never far from her grandfather's call. She retrieved the client folders stashed in the side pockets of her soft leather briefcase. If she wasn't traveling on business, she brought work home every night. After she plopped down on the sofa to read through the files, she pulled her lip ointment from her pocket to moisten her forever-dry lips, then pressed the POWER button on the remote control to watch a twenty-four-hour news station.

She looked at her Swiss watch. Seven o'clock. *Okay, I give.* Riley slid her cell phone from its holder and started to dial then realized she hadn't called Grandpa in a while and couldn't remember his number. Worse, she hadn't bothered to store it in her new camera phone that her brother, John, had sent. She found Grandpa's number in the address book on her laptop, cringing at the thought of waking him. It would be ten o'clock his time.

After the fifth ring, she changed her mind, but before she could end the call, he answered. "Hello?"

Startled by the sound of his voice, Riley hesitated.

"Hello? Who's there?" Her grandfather's agitated tone caused embarrassment to wash over her. She'd woken him. "Riley, is that you?"

She smiled as warmth flooded her. "Grandpa, I'm sorry to wake you."

❧

Unable to sleep, Riley stared at the ceiling in her bedroom. She exhaled and rolled to her side—again. The glowing green numbers of the alarm clock read three thirty. Her grandfather's proposition had thrust her thoughts into chaos. She wondered how she could possibly consider it. She loved him and had heard the desperation in his voice. No one else had any interest in carrying on the family business. Riley's mother had died a year ago, and her aunt lived in Chicago with her family. A few distant cousins lived in the area. They always managed to help with the harvest, but they had high-paying jobs in the city.

Who would take the farm if not her?

Her grandpa had said that he knew she loved the place as he did, and she had her business degree. True, she'd spent much of her childhood at Sanderford Cranberry Farms and managed to be there for harvest as often as possible, taking a week of vacation. But what he asked was a lot—he wanted her to give up her life in California and move to Massachusetts to run things.

Still, she couldn't let go of the idea. If she accepted, she would also have an opportunity to be near her brother, John, and his family, who lived in Plymouth—a short drive from the farm. She'd only learned of his existence two years before, when John had found his biological mother—Riley's mom. Her mother had told her that she'd given up a child for adoption before she was married to Riley's father. Riley's grandmother had not wanted the embarrassment of an illegitimate child. Her church friends would have been aghast.

Riley had always wanted a brother, so she was thrilled when John and his family came into her life. She was so proud of him. A sharp programmer, he had been courted by the National Security Agency to work as a cryptographer. He was fun, too, always leaving her clues to solve some puzzle he'd concocted.

A deep love for John and his family had taken root in her heart—especially for his son, Chad, now two years old. Though it surprised her, she had been overjoyed when John asked her to become Chad's guardian should anything happen to him and Sarah. John's adoptive parents had died years ago, and Riley sensed that Sarah didn't much like her own family.

She glanced at the faint glimmer of the golden letters on her Bible. She needed to pray about this decision and give herself time to consider the possibility. But she felt so far away from the Lord. Weeks had passed since she'd read His Word. With her demanding job, she hadn't made time to meditate on scripture. If she prayed for an answer, would she even hear God over the continual distractions?

Peace eluded her.

Someone pounded on the door to her apartment. Riley

froze. Why would anyone disturb her at this time of night? Her heart raced. She sent up a prayer for protection, hoping that God would hear. The banging continued, forcing her out of bed. She slipped on her robe, crept to the door, and looked out the peephole.

Eric!

Shocked that he stood on the other side of the door, she backed away.

She wanted to throw open the door to give him a piece of her mind for disturbing her in the middle of the night, but she thought better of it. He swaggered back and forth then leaned against the door, mumbling her name as he pounded.

He's sloshed!

"How dare he." She stilled, realizing her mistake. She didn't want him to know she was awake and standing by the door. In fact, for all he knew, she wasn't even home but out of town on business, which was usually the case. A friend could have taken her to the airport.

Panic shuddered through her. She'd tried to end her relationship with him and had finally resorted to ignoring his persistent phone calls. At first, she'd gotten caught up in his career aspirations. But it quickly became clear that Eric was never content. He always wanted more. He wanted more from her, as well, but was unwilling to make a commitment, and she cringed at her own blindness.

Her stomach churned as Eric slammed his fist again. She leaned her head against the door, uncertain whether to answer him in order to tell him to leave. She backed farther away from the door. The man wasn't even a Christian. "Oh, Lord. How could I have let things go so far? Forgive me."

A neighbor's voice echoed through the corridor. She looked through the tiny hole to see who it was. "What's going on here? Can't you see she's not home?" Charles from across the hall stood in his doorway wearing shorts.

"Thank you," she said softly, even though he couldn't hear her.

"Mind your own business, buddy!" Eric slurred; then he disappeared from sight. Riley hoped he had a ride home in his condition.

She opened her door a crack then whispered, "Charles, is he gone?"

Charles had disappeared, as well, but then he burst through his door wearing jeans and a T-shirt. "I'm going to make sure that friend of yours doesn't drive home drunk." He ran through the corridor and down the steps.

Riley closed her door, locked the dead bolt, and stumbled to the sofa. She crumpled, her body trembling as she cried. Eric's behavior was getting out of hand. She wiped her eyes and stared at the pair of gold-framed pictures on the wall, illuminated by the soft glow of a small accent lamp. The one on the right depicted a large palm tree waving in what appeared to be the Holy Land; it read BE STILL AND KNOW THAT I AM GOD. The one on the left portrayed a man looking up into the night sky; it read SEEK THE LORD WHILE HE MAY BE FOUND.

They were cheap, decorative gifts from a friend when she first moved into her apartment. As she stared at the artwork, she realized she'd never even stopped her busy schedule to consider what they said or meant.

Until now.

Despite Eric's intrusion, the question of whether to accept her grandfather's proposal remained at the forefront of her thoughts. She bowed her head and swallowed the knot in her throat. "Thank You, Lord. I think I have the answer before I even asked."

She went back to bed and allowed exhaustion to overtake her.

❧

Riley awoke to the trill of the phone on the nightstand. A glance at the clock told her she'd overslept.

She lifted the receiver. "Hello?"

"Riley?" Her father's drained voice jolted her wide awake.

She sat up in bed. "I'm here. What is it?"

"Your grandfather had me call you. He couldn't stand to give you the news himself. I'm sorry. It's your brother, John. . . . He's dead."

one

Carver, Massachusetts

"Mornin', sleepyhead."

"It's not like we have to milk cows or anything, is it?" Riley rubbed her sleepy eyes and groggily dragged herself through Grandpa's sixties-style kitchen. After two weeks, she was still trying to unpack and settle in and hadn't yet grown accustomed to her grandfather's early hours.

Ding. Her grandfather pressed a button, and the microwave door popped open. The microwave didn't seem to fit in this retro kitchen. He yanked out his coffee cup then proceeded to spoon instant coffee into the steaming water.

"Wouldn't you prefer a cup of freshly ground French vanilla cream?" Riley pushed the START button on the automatic coffeemaker. She should have set it for automatic brew last night but forgot.

"I haven't got any use for that fancy, newfangled coffee." Her silver-haired grandfather grinned at her, producing a wide display of crow's-feet around his still-bright blue eyes. Thick gray brows arched as he puckered his lips to sip the steaming mixture.

Riley turned her back on him and stifled a laugh. She checked the water level on her own coffee. She never waited until it was finished brewing and poured her nondairy creamer into a large I LOVE CALIFORNIA mug, then followed it up with the half cup's worth of coffee brewed so far. She sipped it and turned to lean against the white counter. Her gaze skimmed the kitchen before resting on Grandpa.

No wonder his farm was in poor condition. Grandpa hadn't upgraded anything in over forty years. Well, except for the fact that he'd bought a microwave. He'd kept the farm small, while others had expanded and diversified; some had even grown to handle all of the processing of their produce, whether cranberries or some other crop.

Her grandfather began shuffling pots and pans around in the cabinet, finally producing a large flat skillet. "Bacon and eggs?"

A twinge of nausea rolled in her stomach at the thought of bacon sizzling this early. She covered a yawn and glanced at the clock on the oven as she sat down at the table. Five thirty. "Thanks, but no. I'll just have my granola breakfast bar."

Though Riley's reddish blond hair wasn't quite long enough to stay permanently within the butterfly clip, she attempted to pin it off her neck. She groaned inside because she should be making breakfast for her grandfather, not the other way around. But she wasn't much for cooking, nor was she big on breakfast. She had a feeling a lot of things were about to change.

A blond-haired, two-year-old boy toddled into the kitchen, rubbing his squinting eyes. *They already have.*

"Morning, Aunt Wiley." The sweet syrup of his voice poured over Riley's heart, stirring her love for him and a fierce grief over his loss.

"When am I going home?" He climbed up into her lap, and she lovingly placed her arms around his soft, cuddly body in a tight hug.

Riley's heart felt as if it would break in two at his question. How would she ever explain to him that his parents were never coming back? With sorrow-filled eyes, she looked up at her grandfather, who'd stopped placing slabs of bacon on the skillet. His mouth was turned down, revealing an entirely different set of wrinkles than when he smiled. He returned her stare and nodded his support.

The boy rested his head against her chest, and she caressed it with her chin while struggling for the right words. "I don't know, Chad. Don't you like your room here?" She winced at her completely inadequate answer.

Bacon crackled on the stove. "Sonny boy, would you like breakfast?" Grandpa tried to sound cheery for Chad's and Riley's sakes, but she didn't miss the grief in his tone.

The child lifted his head and shook it. "Ceweal. Don't you have my ceweal?"

Riley ruffled his blond hair. "Of course we have your cereal. You had it yesterday and the day before, remember?"

Her chest tightened with pain when she considered all that had happened in the last few weeks. After attending John and Sarah's funeral, she'd flown back to California and packed her things and moved to Massachusetts to run the cranberry farm and care for Chad.

Riley placed him in a high chair and began gathering a bowl, spoon, milk, and his honey-toasted oat wheels from the pantry. It all seemed surreal as she performed the tasks without thinking. She watched Chad spoon his cereal into his mouth, finding it hard to believe that she was his legal guardian.

When she had agreed to take care of Chad should something happen to John and Sarah, it hadn't entered her mind that their worst fears would come true. They'd been killed in a car accident. Sometimes people experienced a sense of foreboding. Had John felt an impending tragedy? Is that why he'd been so anxious to make arrangements for Chad?

She stood and shook away the grievous thoughts. Despite all that had happened, she was glad she could be here for Chad. And though the farm was in a sad state of affairs, she would do what she could to help her grandfather. That is, if he would listen to her. They'd already had a few heated discussions because he didn't want to move into the twenty-first century. She shook her head. A positive result, though, was that she would be far away from Eric. And maybe, just maybe, she could find a little time to herself. Time with God.

Grandpa crunched his bacon and shoveled scrambled eggs into his mouth. She hadn't noticed when he sat down. "Tell you what," he said between bites. "You go get ready for the day. I'll cut this little boy's hair."

Riley gasped. "You wouldn't dare." She leaned her nose against the top of his blond curls. "I love his hair. Don't you dare touch it."

"He looks like a girl. Needs to look like a man if he's going to live on my farm." Grandpa stiffened as though he realized he might have said too much.

Chad looked at her grandfather over the edge of his cereal bowl, his face contorted. He wasn't yet comfortable with his new home and didn't understand. Riley wondered if he ever would.

She eyed the phone book on the counter. If anything, she needed to get advice about how to explain to a child that his parents were never coming back. "I think it's a good idea, after all. Maybe you could just trim it a little. Nothing dramatic, okay?" She raised her eyebrows in question at her grandfather, making sure to keep the twinkle in her eyes.

Grandpa winked. "After our morning walk, then."

Riley's insides warmed. Her grandfather had gladly included

Chad on his daily walks.

In her room she spent time reading her Bible and talking to God in prayer. After she'd showered and dressed, she grabbed the phone book. She wanted to get started early today, taking inventory of her grandfather's situation by beginning in the office of Sanderford Cranberry Farms. She thumbed through the yellow pages. The ancient phone mounted on the wall shrilled, the sound sending her back to her time on the farm years ago. She let it ring, thinking to let the machine answer it because she needed to get to work.

After the tenth ring, she realized that Grandpa wasn't answering—and neither was his answering machine, because he didn't own one. She laughed and shook her head at the caller's persistence then picked up the receiver. "Hello?"

"Yes, is this the Sanderford residence?" a familiar, smooth male voice asked.

"Um, yes, it is. May I ask who's calling, please?"

"Ms. O'Hare, is that you? This is Zane Baldwyn."

John's business partner.

"We met. . .at the—"

"I remember." She hadn't meant to cut him off.

She recalled his trimmed black hair and cobalt blue eyes. Grief and confusion had been written all over his face. He'd been John's friend for years. The reminder sent an ache through her heart and the acknowledgment that she'd have to make time to talk to him. But not today.

His stiff white shirt and navy designer suit had reminded her of Eric, and she'd felt an instant aversion toward him. She gritted her teeth. It was a premature judgment, but at the moment, she wanted to rid her mind of corporate images. "I'm sorry, I was just heading out the door. I've got a busy day ahead of me. Is there something I can do for you?" Moving from California and adjusting to her new status as a mother had put enormous pressure on her, giving her the sense that if she didn't get on top of things, she'd soon be bogged down by it all.

"Look. I apologize that I approached you at such an inopportune time as a funeral."

She shook her head as she recalled that he'd been tactless, inviting her to lunch as if he were hitting on her—at a funeral of all places. "I forgive you. Anything else?"

"Yes, actually. I really need to speak with you." He hesitated then added, "It's about John, of course. I don't want you to get the wrong idea."

Too late.

"Bernard's at noon?"

This guy was Eric all over again. She had no idea where Bernard's was anyway. "I'm sorry. I really don't have the time today. I've got a child to care for and a business to get familiar with. I've never been a mother before. . . ." Riley covered her mouth, appalled at her babbling. "Can you tell me whatever you need to say over the phone?"

"No. Please, Ms. O'Hare. . .Riley. May I call you Riley?"

Chad came screaming into the kitchen, his hair shaved close to his scalp. Her grandfather followed. Riley gasped. "What happened to his hair?"

"Excuse me?" the voice from the receiver asked.

"I'm sorry, Mr. Baldwyn, I have to go." Riley hung up the phone.

two

Zane Baldwyn slammed the cordless phone into its cradle. "Women!"

Chelsea peeked into his office. "Everything all right, Mr. Baldwyn?"

He'd told the young receptionist months ago to stop chewing gum. The habit was unprofessional. But he could tell by the way she spoke that she'd stored it away in her cheek, probably thinking he wouldn't notice.

"Yes, fine. Thank you." Her question reminded him that he needed to close his door if he wanted privacy. John had left his office door open the night he'd died in the car accident, enabling Zane to overhear a message he left for his sister, Riley. Though he didn't know what good the information would do him if he could never talk to her.

"I don't know. Sounds like you're having girl trouble to me." Chelsea began chewing her gum again, apparently having forgotten Zane's request.

He sent her his practiced none-of-your-business look— the one he'd used countless times in the past on meddling employees in previous companies—because he was afraid his words would come out too harsh to the inexperienced recent high school graduate. She stopped in midchew to look down at the files she clung to; then she tapped them with her long, red fingernails.

"I'd better get busy on these." She disappeared from the doorway.

He'd often heard her talking about her dates. Maybe she could help, after all. "Wait, Chelsea." Zane sprang from his chair to follow her.

She rushed back through as he exited, and they collided, scattering the files over the deep maroon carpet. He could tell by the blush on her face that she might have a crush on him.

Great. He had planned to ask her about how to meet with a woman who wasn't interested in him. But now he wasn't so sure that was a good idea.

"Here, let me help you with those." Zane dropped to the floor to scoop up files with Chelsea.

The girl giggled. "Oh, thanks. I'm really sorry. I heard you call my name, and I was just coming back when—"

Zane held up his hand to stop her. "Chelsea, it's okay. Really. Completely my fault."

She batted her eyelashes and began smacking her gum. Zane paid close attention so that he would not accidentally touch her hand in the process of picking up the files. On second thought, maybe it would be a good idea to stifle any ideas that Chelsea might have about him.

"The reason I called you is that I changed my mind. I do, in fact, need to discuss something not of a business nature," he said.

Chelsea slowed her chewing. An expectant smile lifted her flushed cheeks.

Oh no. This wasn't going as he planned. "There's a woman."

Her brown eyes peered into his. They were both on their knees, picking up files. Her face was entirely too close. Did he imagine a slight pucker on her lips?

Beads of sweat popped out on his forehead. "Another. . . uh. . .woman."

Her lips formed into a slight frown, almost pouting, and

she returned to the task of retrieving papers and files.

"The truth is. . .well. . .I'm not very good with women. There's someone I'm trying to meet for lunch, and she turned me down. What can I do?"

Chelsea finished picking up the files, and Zane stood along with her. He handed the manila folders over. "Mr. Baldwyn, I'm not sure why any woman wouldn't want to go out with you."

Zane's neck grew warm, and he tugged at his collar. "Well, thank you, Chelsea. I don't know what to say."

He strolled with her into the reception area of Cyphorensic Technologies. The luxury office suite had been his decision. In his opinion, the impressive mahogany-paneled walls depicted success.

With his business savvy and John Connor's programming skills, he'd been convinced there was nothing to stop them. Now Zane believed he'd made a horrific mistake in inviting John to leave his stable, well-paying job to partner with him. He'd pounded himself with guilt day and night, wondering if John would still be alive today if he had stayed at his corporate job.

Even if he had not died in the accident, Zane knew that John's marriage had suffered from the long hours he spent developing software for the company. Pain shot through his stomach, and he placed his hand over his midsection. He needed an antacid.

"Mr. Baldwyn?" Chelsea broke through his thoughts. She'd shuffled behind her desk now and gazed up at him with sad puppy eyes. "I'm sorry about Mr. Connor. I know that has to be what's been bothering you."

"Thanks. I apologize if I've not been myself."

Zane stared down at the blond-streaked brunette. She wore too much makeup to his way of thinking. He felt sorry for her. With all that had happened, he had no idea if he would be able to keep her employed. They had no business to speak of yet. But Zane had been wooing his prospects.

"That's all right. I understand. Now, about this woman you're interested in. You really like her, don't you?" She grinned at him like a Cheshire cat.

An image of John's sister, Riley, played across his mind. Zane had never met her in person before the funeral, but John had recently displayed her picture in his office, even proudly placing it on his desk, which was usually off-limits to anything but his computers.

He chuckled. After Zane's two attempts at talking to Riley, he decided her personality was sorely lacking in warmth. "I'm not sure that I like her. I don't even know her." He leaned against the desk. "Tell me. What do you suggest I do?"

"Well, if she won't go to lunch with you, find a reason that you have to talk to her or be with her. It's hard to know exactly because I don't know the specifics."

Zane stared at Chelsea. Of course he had an important reason to speak to Riley. That's why he had invited her to lunch. Then it dawned on him. "Chelsea, you're a genius."

He was thinking in terms of business prospects. He didn't need to do lunch with her. He only needed to go to the cranberry farm to speak with her.

"Oh, Mr. Baldwyn, you're just saying that. But you know what I'll do? I'll pray for you." She smiled up at him; then the phone rang, and she answered. "Cyphorensic Technologies. May I help you?"

Zane took that as his cue to leave and headed back to his office. *Pray for me?* He stifled his laugh until he'd closed his office door. "Crazy girl." Did God actually answer prayers? Did He care about everyday life?

Zane pulled open the top drawer of his desk to grab his car keys then reconsidered. He paced across the Persian rug centered in the room. If he appeared at Sanderford Cranberry Farms, he'd need to have a very good reason. He couldn't just tell her that he'd overheard something he shouldn't have.

Maybe he did need Chelsea to pray, after all. Her proclamation brought a smile to his lips. He hadn't considered praying in years, since he was a child, even. His mother had been consistent in her efforts to make sure he attended Sunday school and church. But that was where it all ended. He'd made himself into what he was today, no thanks to God.

He hurried out of his office and into John's, flipping on the light as he strode through the door. John's desk sat near the far wall, a computer credenza behind it. Pain gripped his stomach again, a manifestation of his grief at having lost his business partner and friend. He eased into John's chair as if it were sacred. There had to be something in John's office—a memento that he could deliver to Riley, giving him the excuse he needed to speak with her. Then he would know whether or not to broach the subject of the phone call.

Zane tried to rub the tension from his neck and face. It was no use. What difference did his knowledge of the call make anyway? Without a programmer to write the software, Cyphorensic Technologies could not continue forward. He'd been a vice president for a software company for years. But it had been a constant battle to do things his way. So he'd gone to work for another company as the CEO. Only this time the board of directors blocked his decisions. Zane started Cyphorensic so that no one could tell him how to run it. He'd funded the entire thing himself, planning for the months it could take before the company began to stand on its own.

Zane wasn't a programmer. But he couldn't let the company

fall apart. As much as he hated to think of replacing John, he needed to hire a programmer as soon as possible. The new employee would not be a partner this time. Zane hoped he would find someone who could pick up where John had left off.

Zane spun around in the Aeron chair—the only chair for hard-core programmers, John had insisted. He stared at John's special desk system, all designed for maximum efficiency, free of clutter and knickknacks. His laptop briefcase remained where Zane had seen him place it. The man was relentless, planning to stay late the night he died. But Zane had insisted otherwise because John needed to focus on his wife, his marriage.

Two more monitors sat on a table nearby, everything networked seamlessly. But John had preferred his laptop. Zane opened the black canvas case to pull out the lightweight computer. Though he'd not spent the countless hours that John had invested in writing thousands of lines of code, Zane knew enough to understand the documentation John placed within his program, explaining each segment. He unzipped the middle section of the case.

His heart skipped. No laptop. He stuck his hand down into the dark case, just to be certain he wasn't missing something. Nothing. He laid the briefcase on top of the credenza and leaned back into the chair, his hand over his mouth. He spun around again to face the desk.

A wireless mouse rested on a brown leather computer sleeve. Zane had mistaken it for a mouse pad at first. He sighed his relief and opened the sleeve. No laptop. He placed his elbows on the desk and rested his head in his hands as he tried to recall the events as they happened.

John had closed the laptop, pulled the cords and wrapped them up, then stuck it all in the laptop briefcase. Zane had stood on the other side of the desk and watched him, reminding him that he shouldn't take his work home with him. He didn't want his friend to do anything to further jeopardize his marriage for the sake of Cyphorensic. Zane had escorted him out to the parking lot and watched him drive away to pick up his wife for a romantic dinner.

Zane's heart pounded, and his breathing grew rapid. He jumped up and tore over to the other computers. Except for the monitors, the hardware was gone.

He slid his cell from his pocket and phoned Sarah's mother, who'd been named the estate executor, to question her about any computers in John's house. John had promised Sarah he'd keep his work away from home. And true to John's word, he'd done just that. All computers remained here, at Cyphorensic.

Not good.

He gasped in disbelief.

John's words to his sister echoed in Zane's mind. . . . *"Riley, are you there? . . . Listen, I sent you something. Watch for it. It's important."*

As John hung up the phone, and before Zane entered his office, John had said, "It might be a matter of life and death."

As the words of that night reverberated in his head, Zane's pulse hammered. What had John gotten himself into? Whatever it was, it appeared to involve Cyphorensic Technologies' software, hence the stolen hardware. He yanked the phone to his ear and started to dial the police.

Wait.

He replaced the receiver. The last thing he needed at this juncture of the start-up company was to tie up Cyphorensic in some sort of technoscandal. John had some prior illegal cyber dealings, but he'd come clean. Zane trusted him. But what if something had changed?

His gut told him that whatever John had sent to Riley was related—maybe he'd even sent the software itself in an effort to keep it safe. Zane had to find out if Riley had received whatever John sent her.

Forget finding a memento to take to Riley. He rushed through the plate glass door of his fledgling company, ignoring Chelsea's questioning calls, and hurried to his luxury car, sliding into the tan leather driver's seat. As he turned the key in the ignition, he clenched his jaw in resolve. The suspicion that had bothered him since John's accident wrapped around his mind, growing stronger. Something was amiss in the circumstances surrounding his partner's death.

Zane clenched the steering wheel. He had to find out what his partner had deemed a matter of life and death and had sent to his sister. He floored the gas pedal and headed to Sanderford Cranberry Farms somewhere on Cranberry Highway.

three

Riley held Chad in her left arm and one of the inspirational pictures she'd brought from California in the right. It would serve as a daily reminder of her new life of peace. She almost laughed out loud. So far, things had been anything but peaceful.

She followed Grandpa through the door of the small, one-room cottage that served as the main office of Sanderford Cranberry Farms. He set a laundry basket full of Chad's toys and a blue-jean quilt on the floor. Riley released her squirming nephew and placed the picture on top of a stack of boxes.

Grandpa flipped on the fluorescent lights while Riley opened the window shades. Give her sunshine over artificial lighting any day of the week. She smiled. After all the time she'd spent working in the skyscrapers of corporate America, that should become her new motto.

Though large maple and oak trees shaded the old structure, as she looked though the window, she had a clear view of the acres of cranberry beds, including the new ones that Grandpa worked to prepare.

The familiar light gray monolithic computer sat like a fossil on the corner of an old aluminum desk.

"When was the last time you turned this thing on, Grandpa?" Riley shoveled around the stacks of papers and musty cardboard boxes, stubbing her toe against one of the taupe filing cabinets. She pressed the POWER button on the vintage CPU. The slumbering machine hummed and churned, beginning to boot up.

Grandpa released a deep sigh. "I'm trying, Riley. It was part of my plan to grow the farm—get modernized. But I've struggled with using the thing. Millie from the church was coming for a while to get it running. She tried to enter information into the accounting software she took the liberty of buying for me, but she said it was too slow. And your brother's wife, Sarah, looked at it for me. She said she'd come back to help me, and she did spend one morning that next week. She said I needed a newer computer, though."

"Well, no kidding. This is a 486 processor."

"It's all Greek to me. And that Millie, I thought she always had her eye on me, even when your grandmother was alive. She offered to help, and, well. . .I was desperate. Makes me feel sick."

"I'm sure that Millie honestly wanted to help you, Grandpa. You shouldn't feel guilty for accepting it." Memories of her grandmother and the time Riley had spent with her making cranberry recipes played across her mind.

"Well, I do. Your grandmother suffered the last few years of her life when the cancer got her." Grandpa lowered himself into a chair on the other side of the desk and stared at his hands. "I can't tell you how much it breaks my heart to lose John and his pretty wife like that, when we'd only just found him. And with your mother gone, too. . . I had hoped that the farm would continue on in the family like it has all these generations." He lifted his gaze to Riley. "But I look around and everyone has gone off to bigger and better things. Your aunt's in Chicago with her family. There's no one left. I thought if I expanded and turned it into something big, like Farrington Cranberries, I wouldn't need to pass it on to family, except I'm too old and too tired to do it."

He sat up and stared at Riley, a big smile forced on his face. "But now you're here."

Riley kept her mouth closed. She wanted to tell him it wasn't possible, but what did she know? "Haven't they moved into all processing, including distribution?"

"Yes. It's crazy thinking, isn't it? The least I could do, though, is increase the business by adding more beds and maybe diversify into something else. I should have done that years ago in order to keep up. I was just set in my ways. I'm not telling you this to disrespect the memory of your grandmother in any way, but her illness. . . Well, it depleted the savings."

"We don't have to talk about this right now if it's too painful." Riley's heart ached for the loss of her grandmother. She hated seeing her grandfather like this. As she watched the monitor come to life, she felt pleased that her grandfather had made the attempt, but she couldn't stand to see him disappointed.

"No," he said, "I need to bring you up to speed. I planned to create more bogs and purchased a dozer to do the job. After I figured how much I would have to pay someone else to do it, well, I realized I could do it myself and bought a 1982 model."

"That's great!" *Over twenty years old?*

"You haven't heard the rest. It has mechanical problems. Worthless. I took out a loan on it, and now with the two bad growing seasons in a row, I'm struggling to pay for the thing." Grandpa frowned. "I should have told you all of this before you committed to come here. I'm sorry."

Riley rushed around the desk to place her hand on her grandfather's shoulder. "No, you did the right thing. Me being here is the right thing." She watched Chad playing on the floor, and her insides rolled with anguish. "We're going to grow this farm. I'm going to help you make it happen. For you. For Chad."

Though the loss of her brother remained at the forefront of her mind, joy surged inside at the thought of building something worthwhile. Chad had lost his parents. He was part of her family now. She wanted to be the best mother she could be, and she would build this business for him. And for her brother.

"Aunt Wiley!" Chad maneuvered his way over to her and raised his arms. She picked him up. He pointed behind her, and she spun around to see a large poster of the Sanderford Farms brand—a huge cranberry stood out in the middle of it. "Cwanbewy?"

"That's right, sweetie. It's a cranberry. We're on a cranberry farm." Chad jumped down and toddled over to touch the picture hanging on the wall, but he couldn't reach it.

Riley turned to smile at her grandfather but continued to speak to Chad. "When I was a little girl, my grandfather used to tell me all about the cranberries. Do you know where the word *cranberry* comes from? Some of the first people to settle our country—the Germans, for one—called it a crane berry at first because when the vines are blooming, they look like a crane. That's a type of bird."

"Cwane?" The child gave his best effort to pronounce the word. Riley thought Chad spoke well for his age.

"That's right. Eventually, the word changed to *cranberry*."

Grandpa winked at her. "He's a bright boy. And I knew you were the one. You always loved the farm so much." He stood and reached for Chad. "I'd better get this little guy out of your hair while you take a look at all the paperwork. I've got chores to do, and he can go with me."

"Thanks. I won't be long. Just want to get organized."

Chad screamed in Grandpa's arms and reached with all his strength back toward Riley. "Oh, all right, you." She took Chad back into her arms and shrugged at her grandfather. "It's no problem. That's why I brought his toys."

Riley didn't want to put Chad into day care. He'd lost his parents, and she wanted him to spend as much time as possible at the farm and with her and Grandpa.

Her grandfather left the office, and Riley put Chad on his quilt to play with his brightly colored toys. She moved behind the desk and surveyed the mess. By the look of things, her grandfather wasn't big on paperwork, but that was no surprise. He'd always loved the outdoors.

The first thing on her agenda was to contact the dozer salesman about his faulty equipment. She shuffled papers and came across the late payment notice, among many others, and finally discovered the seller's name. It took only ten minutes on the phone with the new-and-used dozer dealer, Chuck Sorenson, to learn that he would not change his as-is warranty policy. Still, she could detect no intent in the man to sell broken tractors. It was simply the way of things. He'd given her the phone number of a mechanic.

Chad wandered over as she picked up the phone to dial the mechanic. She offered the boy a piece of chocolate, hoping to distract him, but he wanted both the chocolate and for her to pick him up. She obliged, holding him in her right arm and the phone to her ear in the left. The first opportunity she had to go to town, she would have to purchase a cordless phone. It was impossible to get things done while attached to the desk.

A gravelly voice answered. She pictured the man on the other end covered in grease.

"Yes, I need a mechanic for a 1982 dozer." As Riley waited for the mechanic's reply, she noticed Chad's mouth encircled in brown. She couldn't see his fingers as they gripped her shoulders out of her line of sight, but she imagined them to be chocolate dipped.

"Give me your information. I've got five ahead of you," the mechanic said.

Chad began to whine. Riley shushed him and kissed him on the forehead.

She gave her name and told the man the equipment was at Sanderford Farms on Cranberry Highway. He told her he'd already looked at that dozer and that Robert Sanderford had not been able to pay. Riley's pulse pounded in her ears, along with Chad's whining. Why hadn't Grandpa told her?

She would do her best to negotiate. A knock drew her attention. A businessman appeared in the window of the door.

Riley panicked. What else had Grandpa left out? Was the man a banker or with the IRS? As he reached for the knob, Riley turned her back to him, wrapping the cord around her and Chad. The boy protested. Dread swelled in her chest, and her palms grew sweaty. She shuffled Chad in her arm.

"Listen, Mr.—" The door slammed behind Riley. When the mechanic did not offer his name, she continued. "Mister, I'm desperate here. What if I agree to pay after this year's harvest?"

"Ma'am, I need to be paid for the work. I don't operate like you cranberry farmers. I can't wait until after the harvest when you get paid. I've got a family to feed."

Riley huffed, her mind scrambling for a solution. She whirled around to face the desk again and, too late, remembered she'd turned her back to her untimely visitor.

Oh. Great. Zane Baldwyn. She smiled and motioned for him to take a seat. "I understand. I'll come up with something. You said you'd looked at it already, though. Can you give me your estimate?"

"Give me a minute. I've gotta find it." The sound of a diesel engine revved through the receiver.

Riley acknowledged Zane with a nod. Rather than sitting, he chose to roam around the office, moving and touching things. She stiffened at his boldness and wished the man didn't remind her so much of Eric. He had always been so overbearing, controlling. He had to have his way. Hadn't she told Zane that she wouldn't have time for him today? Yet there he stood, forcing her to see him. She'd come three thousand miles to get away from her ex-boyfriend. But it seemed that he was in the room with her.

Zane turned to look at her as if he knew she'd been staring. She tried to avert her gaze, but his cobalt eyes wouldn't let her. He gave her a genuine smile, though she had the feeling that sorrow over the recent death of her brother dampened it. His clenched jaw relaxed as he looked at her then at Chad. He removed his suit coat and slowly approached as he reached out his hands to the candy-coated boy.

Riley widened her eyes in surprise. She was even more astonished when Chad relinquished his hold on her and scrambled into Zane's arms. He strolled around the office, uncaring that Chad was a detriment to his starched white shirt. Amazing. He cooed and soothed the child. Riley wanted to slap her forehead. Of course Chad would know Zane.

The mechanic returned to the phone and told her his price. She gasped and said thank you then hung up the phone. When she returned her attention to Zane, Chad was asleep in his arms.

Unexpectedly, warmth flooded her heart.

four

With Chad nestled in his arms, Zane watched Riley. Her face had been pale as she hung up the phone but had transformed into an expression Zane couldn't read as she glanced at Chad. Had he offended her by taking the boy? She opened her mouth to say something but hesitated, shuffling papers on the desk instead.

"Mr. Baldwyn. What a surprise." She finished repositioning various-shaped white and yellow papers, then stacked them in a neat pile.

"I see that I've interrupted something important. My apologies." He motioned toward the quilt on the floor to indicate his desire to lay Chad on it. "May I?"

His question seemed to jolt Riley from her somber mood, and she skirted the desk. "Yes, of course. Here, let me take him." Her hands touched Zane's chest as she attempted to wrestle the boy from him. "I'm sorry I didn't think to put him down myself."

Zane edged away from her. "No, I've got him. I can do this."

Riley placed her hands on her hips, appearing a little incensed. But then she relaxed and gave Zane a lopsided grin. "Thank you." She looked at the floor as if the words were difficult to say. "I appreciate you watching him like that."

"Not a problem." Zane bent down with Chad and gently placed him on the quilt. Once certain that Chad would remain asleep, he stood and faced Riley again.

He'd been angry and frustrated when he realized the

computer hardware—all of John's work and the future of Cyphorensic Technologies—had been stolen. He rushed out of his office to get here without finding an excuse to talk to her. As she looked at him, he realized he didn't have a clue how to broach the subject.

Of course he didn't need an excuse. He could simply come out and tell her he'd overheard John's message. Confront her. But she might not be willing to confide in him, a complete stranger to her. For all he knew, she could be part of the problem. He scratched his head and avoided her gaze while he considered what to say.

A picture rested on top of a box, and he picked it up, examining it while he gathered his wits. It read SEEK THE LORD WHILE HE MAY BE FOUND. The notion unsettled him. Zane put the picture back in its place. He should have calmed down before coming here. He must find out what Riley knew, if anything, and if she'd found the item—a password, a program or file, or what, he didn't know—that John had sent to her.

As he opened his mouth to voice his question, he noticed something about Riley that had escaped his attention before. He couldn't be sure, but the Riley in front of him was somehow different than the Riley in the picture in John's office. Interesting.

Strawberry blond hair struggled to escape her apparent attempt to pin it away from her face. The Riley in John's office had straight blond hair. He didn't believe it was a simple matter of hair coloring; even the face was slightly different. He would have to examine the photo to be certain.

"Um, the reason I stopped by is. . . Let me start over." *Man, you're bungling this.* He was an executive, an entrepreneur. Why was he stumbling over his words?

"Yes? I'm waiting. I've got a lot to do. . . ." Moisture appeared in her eyes. Her day didn't appear to be going too well. She turned away from him to squeeze between boxes and filing cabinets in order to get behind the old-fashioned desk, though not the sort of antique that would be worth anything.

It was then he noticed the chocolate smeared over the shoulders of her white T-shirt. He grabbed a tissue out of the box on her desk and handed it to her. Too late, he realized his blunder. He hadn't meant to embarrass her.

"Thank you." She took the tissue from him and wiped her eyes. "I'm sorry. It's been a hard day. I didn't realize it was so obvious."

Zane knew his sudden appearance in her office didn't help matters. He probably only reminded her of John. He took another tissue from the box and moved around the desk, wanting to laugh at the horrified expression on her face. "Turn around."

"What—what are you doing?" Her jade eyes peered up at him. He couldn't be certain, but he thought he saw fear and anger raging behind them.

"I'm not going to hurt you. I simply want to wipe the chocolate off your shirt. It's a really nasty habit, you know."

Realization dawned on her face, and she laughed and showed him her back.

"Chocolate, that is. I take it you're an addict, have a problem." He wiped at the brown splotches then decided the tissue wasn't the answer. "Have you got any water?"

She turned back to face him. "Really, this isn't necessary. I'll have to spray it with stain remover. You talk like you know about chocolate; don't you know it stains?"

"I do; that's why it's imperative that we remove it immediately." Zane spotted the wipes on top of the filing cabinet and pointed. "Those—they'll do." Before he could move, Riley dashed around the desk as if uncomfortable in close proximity to him. Her presence had an odd effect on him. She had single-handedly subdued his anger.

Riley lifted the container. "Empty. But I've got diaper wipes. They'll work."

While she rummaged through the diaper bag, he allowed his gaze to roam over various statements and late notices. It wasn't enough that her brother had died. She also had to deal with this mess.

Riley yanked a wipe out of the box and held it up, her eyes full of mischief. "If I were you, I would worry about the chocolate on my own shirt."

A smile erupted on his face, and he felt it all the way into his heart—a surprising but pleasant sensation. "This old thing? I'll just toss it."

Laughter gushed from her, the sound a symphony to his ears. The telephone rang, discharging the magic of the moment. Zane put his hand on the handset, considering answering it.

"No. I'll get it." Riley furrowed her brows, a warning in her eyes as she rushed to the desk. She stuffed the wipe into his hand before she yanked the annoying device to her ear. "Sanderford Farms."

Reprimanded, he made his way to the chair on the other side of the desk, feeling like a nuisance while he listened to her conversation. He could tell his presence made her uncomfortable.

Cranberry farming. An idea began to formulate in Zane's mind. He closed his eyes and smiled, tuning out Riley's phone conversation. He enjoyed it when things seemed to fall into place like so many carefully placed dominoes. And things were falling into place.

Sitting in the Sanderford Cranberry Farms office relaxed him. He'd overreacted. He decided that he would inform the police of the hardware theft, after all. His strong suspicion that John's death was more than a coincidence was just that— a strong suspicion—probably not enough to convince the police of foul play. He doubted the police's search for missing hardware would materialize into a cyber scandal.

Zane stepped outside to make the call to the police. If there was a connection between the computer theft and John's death, Zane needed to find out on his own. He could do that and still protect his unsullied start-up. He returned to the office to find that Riley remained glued to the phone.

Zane didn't feel comfortable with Cyphorensic Technologies going forward until he discovered what had happened to his friend and his wife, and to the software. In the meantime, he needed information that Riley might have. She appeared to be consumed with making a failing business work and did not act at all like someone who held a big secret in the palm of her hand.

Zane was an entrepreneur. He couldn't help but be interested in all the possibilities that could come out of cranberry farming, including a new challenge.

Riley hung up the phone, slamming it a bit harder than necessary. She rubbed her temples.

Zane's chest swelled with admiration for the strong young woman. Add "new mom" to her task list. He hoped he wasn't making a mistake in offering his help, but somehow her vulnerability had penetrated his better judgment. That much he recognized.

She was John's sister. Chad, John's son. Zane owed it to his friend and partner to help his sister make this work. If he discovered what he needed to know in the process, so much the better. He noticed her staring at him and became aware he'd been caught up in his thoughts. He stood.

She folded her arms across her chest and raised her eyebrows. "You know, you never did tell me why you dropped by. I know it wasn't for pleasantries, since you've already stated at the funeral and on the phone that you needed to speak to me. It was important. Remember?"

"I have a proposition for you." John heard Chad begin to squirm on his quilt. He'd have to do quick work, convince her to agree before she had time to reconsider.

Her incredulous expression urged him on. "John talked a lot about the cranberry farm—intrigued me. I'm an entrepreneur; I'd love to help in any way that I can." He stuck his hands in his pockets to hide the fact that he was nervous, an altogether new emotion for him.

"Look, I'm not sure what you have in mind, but this business is family owned and operated. It's not like you can get it ready so that you can take it IPO or whatever it is you do. I know your type." Riley applied ointment to her lips and rubbed them together then tucked the small container back into her pocket.

She would be as much of a challenge as the business itself. Even better. "No, no. You misunderstand me."

"What about your company? How would you have the time?"

Zane peered out a window that was in need of a good scrub and watched a man head to the office. He had to hurry. "I can't do much with the company right now. I lost my key programmer. My only programmer." He turned to face Riley. "But you know that. Cyphorensic is on hold for the moment." Or at least until he decided how to proceed with it. Sensing her rebuff, he continued. "Think of Chad, if not yourself. Let me do this for Chad, for John's memory. I can help you. It's apparent you need assistance."

The door swung open, and Zane flinched. Had he won her over?

The man stepped into the room then removed his straw hat and nodded at Zane. He looked at Riley. "Ma'am. I've already spoken to Mr. Sanderford, and he told me to come speak to you since you're running things now. Sure wish you would've shown up sooner. Thing is. . .I've had to take another job." He lowered his head. "I'm sorry about that. I've got two teenage boys starting to drive. That comes with a big insurance bill." The man grinned as if he hoped to ease the tension.

Zane wanted to smile at the timing, but he couldn't. He hesitated before looking at Riley, because he knew the turmoil on her face would affect him.

five

Oh great! The day could not get any worse. Riley steeled herself against an onslaught of tears growing behind her eyes. She would not allow herself to break down. "I'm really sorry to hear that, Mr. Finickes, is it?"

She'd only met the man a few days before, but her mind was in overdrive, trying to grasp her new responsibilities plus all the changes that had happened in her life in such a short time.

"Can you give us two more weeks?" She held her breath.

The farm helper looked at his hat. "Ma'am, I'm sorry. My new employer needed someone starting this week. If I want the job, I've got to start now." He looked up at her, regret in his expression.

"I understand. Tell you what. I know we probably owe you something. Why don't you come by tomorrow, or later in the week when you get the chance, and I'll have a check ready for you." Riley could sense Zane watching her, and it unnerved her.

He'd made a valid offer to help with the farm, but she felt pressured and did not appreciate his interference. She could do this job herself, though Mr. Finickes didn't have the greatest timing in the world.

"Thank you, ma'am. Later on this week, then." He placed his hat back on his head, stood tall, and smiled at her before exiting with an added bounce to his step.

Riley opened desk drawers and shuffled through pencils, paper clips, business cards, and an array of disorganized junk, looking for a bottle of painkillers. A sticky blue substance covered her fingers, and she looked for the source. A leaking ink pen. She wiped at the goop with a tissue but only succeeded in smearing the ink, which left a stain.

The pounding in her head began to increase in intensity, and if she didn't stop it soon, she could be facing a full-blown migraine. The bills and late notices drew her gaze as though they screamed at her, demanding her attention. Unsuccessful in her search, she sighed as she closed the drawer and returned her attention to Zane.

"You know, I appreciate your offer. I really do. But I can handle this on my own. It's a great opportunity for me." If she could make it work, that was. She could think of nothing worse than failing and adding to Grandpa's disappointment.

Chad stirred on his blanket and sat up, his pudgy cheeks red. He squinted then rubbed his eyes. "Mommy?"

Pain shot through Riley's tender heart at his words, and she shared a look with Zane. His gaze spoke volumes to her that he cared deeply for the child. She rushed to Chad and picked him up. "No, sweetie, Mommy's not here. It's Aunt Riley."

The inadequate words caused her to frown. For Chad's sake, she wished she could become his mother; then he wouldn't have to grapple with a situation he couldn't understand. She'd not had the opportunity to call a counselor for advice yet, though she would probably speak to the pastor at her grandfather's church as he had suggested.

"Here, honey, let me get you some juice." The yellow top of a sippy cup protruded from the elastic side pocket of his diaper bag. She pulled at it, but the bag wouldn't relinquish its hold.

"Allow me." Zane pulled the apple juice out and handed it over to Chad, who smiled at him. It was obvious the boy returned Zane's affection.

She understood why Chad loved him so much. He was kind and considerate. "I should probably get back to work, Mr. Baldwyn, and I'm sure you've got something you must do, as well. Again, I appreciate your offer, but I can handle this." Riley hoped she sounded convincing; the pressure in her head was mounting, and she didn't have an inkling how to get on top of things now that Chad was awake.

Zane jammed his hands into his pockets and paced. "May I ask you a question?"

Though his manners were endearing, the man couldn't take no for an answer. She gritted her teeth to contain her frustration. After her experience with Eric and now Zane, Riley began to wonder if all men were bullheaded.

"Go ahead."

"Don't think me rude, but how do you plan to run this business and take care of Chad?" He pinned her with a blue-eyed stare.

She bristled and opened her mouth to speak, but he held up his palm to stop her. "Let me at least help you get organized, get things running smoothly. It's what I do. I can see that you've come into an impossible situation."

Zane pulled his other hand out of his pocket and moved close to Riley. "I feel like I need to do something for John, for his son and sister. Don't deny me this." He leaned in and kissed Chad on the cheek.

The tender kiss startled her. She stiffened at his nearness. His cologne fogged her thinking, and she backed up to clear her mind.

"What do you know about cranberry farming? You're a computer geek, for crying out loud." Riley pressed her dry lips together, hoping she hadn't offended him. "When would you have time to do this, and how would you work? Are you even willing to get your hands dirty?"

Zane grinned at her onslaught of questions. Not the effect she'd been shooting for. He unbuttoned his left shirtsleeve and began to meticulously fold it over until it reached his elbow. Then he started on the other, again taking time to be precise with each crease.

"First of all, I'm not a computer geek. Your brother was, remember?" His smile faded at his mention of John. He placed his hands on his hips. "I'm ready to get my hands dirty. I'll work part-time in the morning for a few weeks, months, however long it takes. I'll take care of Cyphorensic and other business in the afternoon."

He came across as ridiculous, standing there with his sleeves rolled neatly to his elbows, yet his starched white shirt looking as though it had been painted by an artist working in chocolate. Riley covered her mouth to hide her smile.

He raised his arms in question. "What? You don't believe me?"

"So you're really going to just throw that shirt away?"

Zane's eyes widened; she'd caught him off guard. He looked down at his shirt as if seeing Chad's artwork for the first time and laughed.

His laughter sent an unexpected thrill through her heart. She'd been wrong. Zane was not like Eric. Her ex-boyfriend would never have the desire or need to help anyone—unless he had an ulterior motive. Still, she'd been a poor judge of character in the past and couldn't be certain of Zane's intentions. She cradled Chad in her arms, desiring to focus on the child and, for the moment, put aside her concerns about Zane's true reasons for wanting to help.

"All right."

His cheerful expression turned serious, his smile fading. "You won't regret this, Riley. May I call you Riley? I'm not sure we ever established that."

His eruption of words made her dizzy. "Yes, yes, you can call me Riley."

᠑

As Zane pulled into the parking lot of the two-story business complex that housed Cyphorensic Technologies, he tried to relax. He'd made the decision to help Riley on the cranberry farm in order to search for what John had sent her, or at least to earn her trust so that she would tell him. But while he was in the farm office, he couldn't think of anything he wanted to do more than help her. He owed that much to John. But he had to admit it wasn't the best business decision he'd ever made. Against his better judgment, he'd offered to spend time organizing things and getting the farm ready for expansion. All he'd really needed to do was be forthright and ask her about John's message.

He slammed the car door and pressed the security alarm button on his key fob as he headed toward the building. Something about Riley, her desperate need, or possibly the combination of Riley holding Chad and her desperate need, had touched his heart. Awakened it. Made him feel alive. It astounded him that with everything he'd done with his life, he'd never felt this way before. And he wanted to feel this way more.

Zane stared at the gold-etched name of his lifeless company; then he pushed through the plate glass doors of Cyphorensic Technologies to see Chelsea stashing personal items into a cardboard box. He stopped in the middle of the small lobby. "What are you doing?"

She curved her lips without flashing her usual bright smile. "Mr. Baldwyn, sir, you don't need me. There's nothing going on here. Hardly anyone ever calls. And except for when

Mr. Connor was still alive, well, no one stops by anymore. I wanted to be a receptionist so I could see people. I love people. I've filed everything there is to file. Twice."

She smacked her gum in sheer freedom. "Besides, I got a new job. I'll be working for a veterinarian. I love animals. Oh, and I almost forgot. The police are here. I didn't know that Mr. Connor's computers were stolen, but I showed them his office."

Zane hesitated, absorbing her news as he stared at her. He hadn't noticed any cruiser in the parking lot. "They're here?"

"They only just showed. They're looking around Mr. Connor's office, taking pictures and prints, I think." She cleared her throat. "The investigating officer said he needed to ask you questions. He's so cute."

Zane sighed. "Well, I'm here now." He headed back to John's office.

"Mr. Baldwyn. Glad you could make it." One of the two uniformed officers greeted him with a smile. "I'm Sergeant Draper."

"Sorry I'm late. I phoned in not that long ago. Figured it would be awhile before anyone showed."

The officer's smile flattened, but he maintained his friendly, relaxed stance. He proceeded to question Zane regarding the theft. Zane answered with the facts, leaving any of his qualms out of the equation. No need to introduce his theories at this point.

"Your alarm system's been disabled. I suggest you invest in something that can't be disabled through the simple cutting of wires."

The information startled him. Had setting the alarm become such a rote operation that he'd failed to notice the system hadn't armed? "Thanks. So what happens next?"

"There's been a rash of electronic thefts in the area lately. TVs, stereos, and computers. Unless you have something else to add..."

Zane shook his head. What was he going to say? His partner had died in a car crash a month ago but had sent something he thought might be a matter of life and death to his sister? He'd had a nefarious history of hacking? "I need to take some files home. That's okay, isn't it? I'm a workaholic."

"I think we have all we need." Sergeant Draper nodded his dismissal of Zane and headed out of John's office along with his partner.

A rash of electronic thefts. Zane tugged at his collar. Was he being paranoid to think that the stolen hardware had anything to do with John? Still, there was his strange comment about life and death....

Zane stood in the hallway and watched them stroll through the reception area. Chelsea's smile brightened. Sergeant Draper lingered longer than necessary before leaving. Once the officers were gone, Zane approached Chelsea. She resumed stacking various pictures of family members and friends into the box next to something pink and fluffy that Zane didn't recognize. He knew she was right, of course. There was no reason for her to remain at Cyphorensic. She was a vivacious, attractive young woman and needed interaction.

"I mean, if things were busy, I wouldn't leave you. You could count on me. But except for Mr. Connor's client, well, you don't need me."

Zane froze. "What did you say?"

Chelsea stopped chewing and gave him a look that said she thought he was old and losing it, apparently forgetting her earlier infatuation with him. Zane knew she hadn't intended to appear that way, but it cut him nevertheless.

"I said you could count on me if things were busy. . .if you needed me." She went back to smacking, even attempting a bubble. "But you don't."

"You said something about Mr. Connor's client." Zane didn't want to sound as though he wasn't aware of any clients. Probably Chelsea had misunderstood.

"There was that one man who came to meet with Mr. Connor. Twice, I think. I told him that you were out of town, but he insisted on meeting Mr. Connor."

Fire seared Zane's stomach, and he groaned.

"Are you all right?" Chelsea reached out to touch his shoulder.

"Yes, fine, thanks. I just need to get my antacid. The twenty-four-hour stuff isn't any match for my ulcers. I need the name of Mr. Connor's client so I can contact him and let him know what happened, that John died in an accident."

Chelsea's face went pale. "I—I don't know his name. He didn't give it. I'm so sorry. I'm a lame receptionist, aren't I?" She plopped into her seat and looked at him for validation. Zane feared she would cry.

"It's all right, Chelsea. No need to be upset." *The only person who ever came through the doors and you failed to get his name?* "What can you tell me about this man? Who did he work for?"

She looked up at him, stricken. "If I knew that, don't you think I would have gotten his name?"

Zane could only frown at her. He couldn't conjure a smile, even for Chelsea. "Quite right. Well, I guess this is good-bye, then. I wish you well." Frustrated, he moved to head to his office.

"Mr. Baldwyn?"

He stopped and turned to face her again. "Yes?"

"I can tell you the man sort of scared me. He had black hair and wore an expensive-looking black suit, kinda like you do, only you usually wear blue or dark gray."

"Scared you?"

She nodded.

"Why did he scare you?" Chelsea was inexperienced. She was being melodramatic.

Eyes closed, she paused as if in deep thought. "I have a photographic memory. Did I ever tell you that? I can see him in my mind right now. Well, for one thing, he wasn't warm and friendly. Usually people are friendly to me. Oh, oh. And I remember Mr. Connor wasn't pleased to see him, at least at the office."

Heat rushed up Zane's neck. "Did Mr. Connor actually say that?"

Chelsea's cheeks reddened enough to be seen through her heavy makeup. "Um. . .yes. I'm sorry. I overheard him."

"Thanks for the information. If you think of anything else, I'll be in my office or Mr. Connor's."

He left the reception desk and hurried down the hall to John's office. He rummaged through the desk drawers, searching for anything that would tell him who John's visitor had been. For all he knew, it could have been a friend. The way that Chelsea presented it, the man had been a client. Still, he wasn't Zane's client and John hadn't mentioned him.

Nothing was safe here—that is, if the thieves had left anything. Zane retrieved empty boxes from a spare room they'd used as storage and began packing anything that appeared important from John's office. They'd taken the computer hardware and all of the storage media. Zane stashed manila folders, hoping they would contain hard copy of pertinent information, into the boxes.

He went through the same drill in his own office and stuck the boxes in the dark corridor. He hadn't realized it was so late and flicked on more lights as he went back to John's office to make sure he hadn't missed anything.

Then he saw it.

The picture of John's sister, Riley, sat on the desk in a small bronze frame. He examined the photo closely. He was right. She looked very different in this photo, and his gut told him that it wasn't her. Yet John had said it was his sister. Zane placed it on top of the files in a box and headed out the door to load his car.

With all the boxes secured in the trunk and on the seats of his car, he hurried back to switch off the lights and lock the doors. When Zane returned to open his car door, movement in his peripheral vision caught his attention. He looked at the corner of the building to see a shadow skate into the darkness.

Zane jumped into his car and sped out of the parking lot. If he wasn't convinced before that John's death had been no accident, he was now. Since the thieves were still lurking around the office, then perhaps they had not retrieved what they were searching for. That put Riley and Chad in danger, as well. He took comfort in the fact that she'd allowed him to work with her. At least he would be on hand if protection was required.

After bringing the boxes up to his condominium and stacking them in his home office, Zane swiped the photo of Riley out of the box and found a lone soda in the sparse refrigerator. It would be a long, grueling night, but he needed to get started searching through the documents if he was to make any sense of it all.

He reclined on his navy blue leather sofa and gazed at Riley's photo while he sipped, the carbonation burning his throat as it went down. No, the woman in this picture was not Riley. Warm images of the feisty woman he'd spent the morning with floated through his tired mind.

six

A bright blue sky promised a glorious day and, Riley hoped, a better one than yesterday. She covered a yawn as she carried Chad, who was still sipping on his cup of milk and wearing footed pajamas, to the Sanderford Farms office. The structure rested across the circular drive from Grandpa's farmhouse.

Zane's sleek, black luxury car was parked in front. Her heart skipped a beat. The unexpected reaction to seeing he'd arrived early aroused mixed emotions, and she couldn't decide if she should smile or frown.

She'd wanted to spend time with Zane going over Grandpa's plans for expanding the farm and had counted on Grandpa taking Chad for the morning. But he'd mentioned working on the pumps for the irrigation system and left early. He must have unlocked the office door for Zane. Since she'd agreed to allow him to assist in the business, she would have to remember to give Zane his own key. She pressed her lips to Chad's forehead and tousled his already mussed-up hair then opened the office door.

Zane stood behind the desk, holding a spray bottle and cloth, dressed in a cream-colored sweater and blue jeans instead of a designer suit like he'd worn the two times she'd seen him. He looked up from orderly papers and files and sent her a brilliant, heart-stopping smile.

"Good morning, Riley." His blue eyes glistened with warmth as he moved around the desk in one fluid motion.

Riley shut the door behind her and clung to the knob as if

it would give her strength to fight the strange weakness in her legs. "You've been busy."

"How's my boy this morning?" Zane reached out his arms, and Chad allowed Zane to take him. He rested his head on Zane's chest.

Zane scrutinized the child's hands. "What, no chocolate today?"

"Shh." Riley glared at Zane. "You know he understands you, right?"

Chad lifted his head to Riley. "Candy?"

"No, sweetie. Aunt Riley won't make that mistake again. At least not in the office while I'm working."

Chad scrambled down and toddled to his toys left on the quilt from yesterday.

Zane stuck his hands in his pockets. "You know, even the best moms hire babysitters sometimes, that sort of thing. It wouldn't hurt to get help with him. In fact, he might enjoy going to a day care."

His words sounded like an affront to her. She crossed her arms and glowered. "Only yesterday you questioned how I could run the business and give Chad the time he needed. Were you just using that to get your way? I thought you were here to help." Her pulse pounded in her ears.

"Calm down, Riley. I did say that, and I meant it. I wasn't using your predicament with Chad." He shifted closer to her and placed a tanned hand on her arm. "I was merely thinking of you. You looked tired and drained. And Chad would enjoy time with other children. You can still be his primary caregiver."

She turned away from him and took a calming breath to rein in her irritation. The man acted as if he knew more about parenthood than she did. Her incompetence frustrated and embarrassed her. The inspirational picture she'd brought in yesterday remained where she'd placed it, and she held it up to the wall, trying to decide the best place to hang it. "How—how do you know so much about kids?"

"I don't want to give you the wrong impression. I know hardly anything about children. Really." He hesitated as if carefully considering his next words. "I only repeated words that John said to his wife. He told me they'd had marital troubles since Chad's arrival. It seems obvious to me that it would be difficult—things wouldn't be the same. I babysat for them a few times to help. That's why Chad and I are buddies."

Riley whirled to face him again. "No way."

He laughed. "Yes way." A distant look appeared in his eyes, and he frowned. "But then John began working too much, hardly ever went home. He said he needed the extra time because he was in the most intense part of the project." Zane shook his head then focused on Riley. "So how about you? You appear to be experienced with children. I'm impressed by the way you handle Chad."

Riley wanted to hear more about John's work, but she sensed that Zane's intention had been to revert to the original subject. "Babysitting was my business in high school. I was even certified."

"Certified?"

"Yeah, at the local hospital they taught classes that included CPR and offered babysitting certification."

"Well, you know what you're doing. I apologize if I overstepped."

She dismissed his words with a wave of her hand and returned her attention to the picture. "No. It's all right. I think you mean well. Babysitting is one thing. Parenting is totally different, which I'm finding out. It's just that I'm not ready to let anyone else have him right now."

Zane sighed behind her.

"He just lost his mom and dad." Riley's words came out shaky, and she wiped at the sudden tears, grateful she wasn't facing Zane. "Sorry. I miss John."

Zane tried to turn her and pull her into his arms, comfort her, she knew. Riley would have none of it. "No, I'm fine."

Zane handed her a tissue. She breathed deeply, took it, and gave a short laugh. She looked back at the picture.

"This says to be still and know that I am God." She sniffled as emotion continued to batter her insides. "I don't even know if John knew God. Never asked. Can you believe that? I never asked. What kind of Christian doesn't ask her brother if—"

She peered at Zane's speechless expression. "I'm sorry. I didn't mean to have an emotional breakdown on you."

He narrowed his gaze as if in deep contemplation while he stared at the picture. For the first time, it occurred to Riley that Zane might not be a Christian. She hadn't considered it either way until that moment.

He caught her looking at him, and his reverie fell away. "Look, why don't you give me a tour of the farm. You can tell me what you and your grandfather want to do here. I mean, give me the entire picture. I want to know your greatest dreams for this place. That would go a long way in helping me to know what direction to take. Organizing paperwork is one thing. But I love to make things happen."

Once again Zane had changed the subject, but his talk of dreams pleased her. "That sounds like a great idea. I need some fresh air. I'll get Chad's stroller. Do you mind watching him while I run to the house?"

"You know I don't."

When Riley returned with the three-wheeled jogging stroller, she set it on the lawn outside the office. She unlatched the tab to unfold it and yanked on the handle. It snapped into place. She bounded up the steps and opened the door to peek in.

"Chad, I brought you a change of clothes; then we can go for our walk."

Zane sat behind the desk, holding Chad, who pointed at a slim, charcoal-colored laptop computer. He whispered into the child's ear before he looked to Riley and smiled.

"I don't blame you for bringing your laptop. Who could work on that old computer?" She motioned toward the antique slumbering on the side table.

"You're only correct on one count. I can't work on that old computer. On the other, you're wrong. This isn't my laptop. It belongs to Sanderford Cranberry Farms."

Riley's mouth dropped open. She gathered her wits and said, "What are you talking about, Zane? I don't even know that we can afford a new computer right now. We've got other problems. Like a dozer that needs repairing." Though the new laptop thrilled her and she chided herself for sounding ungrateful, Zane had overstepped.

Pleasant voices resounded from the device speakers, causing Chad to giggle. Zane slid him off his lap and onto the chair as he stood. "Relax. They don't cost all that much. I stopped at a twenty-four-hour shopping mart this morning. If it bothers you that much, just consider this the beginning of much-needed cash flow—a loan to help get things moving."

She thrust her hands onto her hips. "I have my own laptop. You should have said something. You could have used mine."

Riley scratched her head. "I was thinking of using it—just hadn't gotten that far yet."

"You think I don't have one I could use? I run a computer software company, remember? If you want to itemize this for your business, it has to be used for business." Zane frowned, his disappointment evident. "You know, I really thought you'd be pleased."

Why couldn't she be happy that he'd taken the initiative? She should have expected that from him, an entrepreneur. Instead, she'd ruined the moment. It astonished her that his hurt expression bothered her as much as it did.

She relaxed and slid her forefinger along the top of the sleek machine. "I'm sorry for making such a fuss. You're right. We do need this. Thank you for thinking of it."

The man amazed her. He'd only spent one morning in her office, and that was to convince her to let him help. He hadn't wasted any time getting to work.

"You worry too much. I know you want this place to be a success for your grandfather. And it will be. Things aren't as terrible as they seem. Show me the farm. I'll work on a tentative business plan. In fact, we won't even wait for the plan to get started on things. Like, say, the dozer." Zane raised his eyebrows and tilted his head toward the window.

"You didn't!" Riley rushed to the window to peer out. A tow truck was in the process of hoisting it onto a trailer. Her grandfather stood talking to one of the men. "I take it Grandpa knows and approves."

"Let's see. His words exactly were, 'My granddaughter's as smart as a whip.'"

She jerked her face from the window to stare at Zane, looking for a trace of sarcasm. The warmth in his eyes coaxed her suspicions away.

"He's right. Riley O'Hare has everything under control because she hired a consultant to get things moving," he said then winked.

Her spirit surged with hope. She grinned at him. "I have to admit. . .you're good."

❧

Zane strolled next to Riley as she pushed a napping Chad in a big-wheeled jogging stroller along a dirt path toward the cranberry beds. Her hair appeared lighter in the sunshine. It bounced at her shoulders with each step she took. The breeze swept a few errant strands across her face.

She flashed a smile his way. "I have to be honest with you. With myself. I'm starting to realize that I don't know anything about the business of cranberry farming. I think Grandpa has expectations because I have a business degree. But that doesn't mean anything."

The undeveloped road swerved to the right, and they followed its course. A lush green meadow surrounded by ancient oaks extended for several acres to Zane's left.

"I'm sure you know more than you think," he said.

"I practically grew up here. Lived here most of the time in the summer. Of course, during harvest season, everyone pitched in. But I only saw things from a child's point of view. I came out a few times as an adult. I realize there is much more to running a farm now that I'm living here."

Riley sounded winded, so Zane grabbed the handles. "Here, let me."

She relinquished control and stepped to his side without disturbing their cadence. "I should be in better shape than this. But I haven't exercised in a few months. It's amazing how quickly you can get out of shape."

Zane stared straight ahead, focusing on the road. He'd

noticed Riley's slender, appealing figure. He chided himself for allowing his thoughts about her to veer from anything other than business—something he struggled with, the more time he spent with her.

"I can tell you the basics. My great-grandfather purchased the eighty acres that is now Sanderford Farms. There's only about ten acres producing cranberries, a pond, thirty or forty acres of woodland. I'm not sure on all of the numbers, but Grandpa knows, and he can tell us. Plus there's a reservoir for use with the bogs. It's quite a process. Actually, now that I think about it, Grandpa should be showing both of us all of this. I haven't exactly had the time to refresh myself with the details."

The young woman had already faced quite a challenge, yet she appeared to stand ready to tackle another. Zane felt a rush of admiration for Riley and drew a deep breath.

"Oh, so now you're getting winded. Let me take it, then. We're almost there anyway. Look, you can see the dikes," she said.

They strolled to stand on heaped-up dirt surrounding the cranberry beds. Sprinklers doused the plants with water.

"All that green covered with pink and white flowers you see is the cranberry runners. Surprising how thick they grow, isn't it?" Riley shook her head, her expression bright, beautiful.

Zane scrambled down the dike and stepped over the irrigation pipe to take a closer look. He stared in awe at the millions of shiny red-green leaves, swelling up the runners. "Truly amazing. I've spent most of my time in office buildings, working in front of a computer. I regret that I haven't taken more time to enjoy nature." The fresh air and the vegetation had a calming, therapeutic effect on him. Yet it was Riley's youthful excitement that fascinated him.

"Grandpa started dozing new beds in April. He said it had taken too long because he had to make sure they were level and he wasn't experienced in using a laser level." Riley laughed. "But he's trying."

She continued strolling. "Then he'd spread six inches of clay over them for the first layer. But that's when the dozer broke down. We've still got to put down six to eight inches of organic material like loam or peat, then sand. That'll take weeks, so depending on how long it will take that mechanic you hired to repair our dozer, I think we may miss planting new fields for this season. Even so, any new vines would take at least five years to give us fruit."

Her words stunned him. He hadn't considered that it would take so long; he'd hired a mechanic without doing much research. The news that he'd miscalculated goaded him. "Then why were you trying to hire a mechanic yesterday?"

"What? I'm not saying it's the way things will go. I just don't know. But we can always try. We don't want to lose an entire planting season."

Impatience threatened to rob Zane of enjoying the farm tour and Riley's presence. He felt for his cell in his pocket as he considered the possibility of getting a new dozer.

Chad squirmed, waking up. Riley handed Chad his drink then stood to face Zane. He'd learned his lesson and felt certain that she would not approve of the purchase. With his limited knowledge, it would be an impulsive action at best.

"I think Grandpa wishes he could diversify into every aspect of cranberry processing. But that is beyond the realm of possibility to me."

A chill of exhilaration raced through Zane. It amazed him how the idea of expanding this farm excited him. Riley's jade eyes peered at him as though questioning his thoughts. A slight grin spread over her lightly freckled cheeks. She wore minimal makeup, enough to accentuate her eyes and lips. He thought her face was flushed from the exercise, but the red on her cheeks deepened.

She looked away from him. "I'm not sure what you do and don't know about cranberries. So just ignore me if I tell you something that you already know. But these are not actually real bogs in the true sense. The cranberries have to be dry while they grow in the peat and sand. It's only during the harvest that the bogs are flooded and the cranberries float to the top. That's why they're called bog rubies."

"I didn't realize that. See, you know more than you think."

"Well, I've helped with harvest over the years as often as I could, even after we moved to California. I've been researching on the Internet late at night, too, to help fill in the blanks." She grinned.

Chad threw his cup on the road, and Riley huffed. While she leaned over to pick it up, Zane released the child from the captivity of his stroller. Chad delighted in running in circles.

Zane studied Riley then said, "I know that harvest season is in October, right?"

"Yes, the bogs are flooded. That's when all of the equipment is put into use and the extra workers are needed."

"Well then, we've got some time. It's only the end of June." Zane cringed at his words. He hadn't planned to work here through October. He needed to resolve if and why John was murdered—and find his missing software—before then. If only he knew what he was looking for.

He watched Riley hold hands with Chad as they danced around in a circle, trusting and innocent. He could potentially resolve the mystery if he told her of his suspicion of John's murder and asked her to tell him what John had sent. He'd made a mistake. He should have presented her with his suspicions yesterday, instead of this plan to help her. But it wasn't a scheme; he was genuinely pleased to think of making the cranberry farm an operation that she and her grandfather could be proud of.

If he solved the puzzle surrounding John's death today, he would still want to do that.

But he couldn't stand to think of the outcome of relating his suspicions. The woman juggled too many things already. She didn't need or deserve to have fear heaped onto her already-full plate. An unpleasant thought occurred to him, causing his heart to palpitate. How would Riley react when she learned of his deception? He pushed the anxiety away, out of his mind. No, he would try to discover the truth on his own, protect her for the time being.

John would have sent something ordinary, and only a person aware that the item was a clue to a puzzle would think to engage in solving it. He didn't think Riley had known her brother long enough to be aware of that side of him, but he wasn't sure.

"What are you thinking about?" Her pleasant voice brought him back. "You can't fool me. I see those wheels turning."

She stopped playing with Chad and drew him into her arms then came to stand before Zane. "Something's bothering you. What is it?"

Surprised, he said, "You know me that well already? I need to be more careful."

He turned to face the road back to the house and office. "We should get back."

"But I haven't shown you the equipment or pump."

"I've seen all I need to see for now." He knew his words came out cold, and her confused expression cut him to the core. Though he was connected to Riley and cared about her because she was John's sister, he was beginning to have feelings of a different nature for her. And it scared him. He'd already lost everyone he'd ever cared about.

seven

After lunch, Riley went back to explore the farm. She'd lost track of time, and as a result, they would have to eat a late dinner. While she stored the stroller in the mudroom, Chad wandered through the entryway to the kitchen. She trailed behind him then marched to the sink to wash her hands and splash water over her face.

"Juice, juice. . ." Chad pointed to the plastic apple juice container she'd left on the counter earlier. Only it was empty.

"I'm sorry, it's all gone. How about water?" She filled his cup with the filtered bottled water she'd purchased. Every time she watched Grandpa drink from the tap, she squirmed. She wasn't accustomed to drinking the hard water on the farm.

The child took a sip then threw the cup on the floor, shaking his head. "No. I want juice."

Riley huffed and lifted Chad, hoping to distract him. "How about milk?" She set him in the high chair and buckled him in. "Better yet, how about chocolate milk?" At the moment, she didn't want to risk his discontent with her new suggestion and would try anything to please him.

Tired and frustrated, she allowed her mind to think about her life in California. After a long day, she had time to kick off her shoes and recuperate, even though she had brought work home. Things were different with a child.

She opened the freezer to rummage through its offerings. Grandpa stomped his boots outside before entering the mudroom. He appeared in the kitchen wearing socks, his clothes covered with grease and dirt.

Riley gasped. "Grandpa. You look a mess."

"The irrigation pump's broken. It's beyond repair, so I'm going to need a new one."

She closed her eyes at his statement. Everything was breaking at once. She stifled her desire to ask him if he'd replaced or upgraded anything in all these years. She was here to help, not hurt.

"I've got to get cleaned up. Say, you wouldn't mind popping in a frozen dinner for me, would you?" he asked.

Riley stared at the diminishing contents of the freezer. "You know, I need to do some shopping. I'm sorry that we've been eating everything. I need to share the responsibilities; I just haven't had time."

Though she'd decided to live in her grandfather's house and divide the expenses, she hoped to have a place of her own at some point.

"Grandpa, what do you like to eat?" She glanced at the tray standing by his favorite recliner in the living area. "You can't exist on TV dinners all the time."

"If you want to cook something for you and Chad, I might share a bite with you." He grinned. "Whatever you decide will be fine with me."

After washing his hands with grime-removing soap, he grabbed a glass from the cabinet and filled it with water from the faucet. She would have to encourage him to clean up in the bathroom. Maybe she could talk him into drinking purified water, too.

He emptied the glass then sighed. "You know, your grandmother did all the cooking. I never learned. Since it has been just me here, it hasn't been worth the effort." He headed through the living room and up the stairs to his bedroom.

Great, just great. Not only was she going to raise a child and run a farm; she'd have to learn to cook. She understood her grandfather's sentiment, because she hadn't made the effort to cook for herself much, either, but she'd soon have to pick up the skill. She looked over at Chad, who busied himself with the empty plastic juice bottle he'd somehow managed to reach from the counter.

"I'm sorry, I forgot all about your chocolate milk." Riley retrieved the jug from the fridge and noticed this would be Chad's last cup until she went to the store. Unless, of course, he was willing to accept water. Maybe she could stretch it into two cups if she only poured him half. She stirred in some chocolate syrup, something she kept on hand for stressful moments. After handing the cup to Chad, she poured a spoonful of the delightful syrup and stuck it in her mouth.

She closed her eyes and enjoyed the sweet taste, willing the stress away. "Mmm."

Zane's words about getting help with Chad came back to her as she watched the two-year-old sip with delight. He looked at her, his eyes wide with pleasure.

"Good, isn't it?" she asked.

He nodded.

Her heart ached at the thought that Zane could be right. If only she had a little help with the child, she could get on top of things around the farm. Who was she kidding? She needed to work on more than the business. The boy needed decent, healthy food. Fruits and vegetables. Her shoulders sagged as she leaned against the counter. So far she'd been a complete failure as his guardian.

She hadn't prepared ahead of time for dinner and would have to scramble to pull it together. Then she needed to run to the store. She ran her hand through her hair, thinking she'd give almost anything to take a nice, relaxing shower right now.

Grandpa would go to bed early—because he woke up much too early in her opinion—so she would have to take Chad with her to shop. She reminded herself that he was all she had left of her brother, and she would do whatever it took to make things work. Besides, she couldn't afford child care yet.

Gravel crunched outside. Riley leaned over the sink and looked out the kitchen window. Zane's car pulled to a stop. Her heart jumped with pleasure. She chided herself for her unwarranted reaction. She knew little about him and would have to exercise more self-control over her emotions. Still, it surprised her that he'd returned, and she wondered if he'd forgotten something.

She rushed to the door and opened it. His eyes brightened when he saw her. "Pizza, anyone?" He held up three large boxes.

Relief flooded Riley. "You're a lifesaver. But then, I suppose you already knew that. Come in." She held the door open for him as he entered the kitchen through the mudroom.

He placed the boxes on the counter. The pepperoni pizza steamed when he lifted the lid. "I didn't know what kind you liked or how much to get. But almost everyone loves pepperoni."

"Pizza, pizza!" Chad bounced in his high chair.

"And I already knew that the little guy likes pepperoni. That's what we had when he stayed with me."

Riley couldn't believe her good fortune. "You know, I appreciate this. I can't tell you what great timing this is."

He flashed his smile before grabbing a slice and holding it out to her. "Aren't you hungry?"

"Yes, thanks. Let me grab a few plates first." She retrieved dishes from the cabinet. "Grandpa will be excited. All he ever gets are those frozen dinners. He's cleaning up and should be down in a while."

Riley took a bite. Cheese strung from her mouth to the pizza, unwilling to let go. She saw Zane watching her. Embarrassed, she grabbed a napkin and wiped her mouth.

She sat down at the table, and Zane joined her. They made trivial conversation, chatting about the weather and the next day's agenda. Riley finished her second piece and was about to consider a third when she noticed that tomato sauce covered Chad's face and clothes.

She frowned. "Solving one problem only creates another. He'll have to go straight to a bath after this."

"Maybe not," Zane said. "I usually just wipe him up with a wet washcloth, and then he's good to go. I mean, I would hate to think that I only created more work for you." Teasing glimmered in his eyes.

"No, no. That's not what I meant. But I do have to ask, why did you come back? Why the pizzas?"

"Well, I felt bad for the way I rushed out on you today. I had things I needed to take care of. I thought we could talk more about the business—get to know each other better in a more relaxed atmosphere. You know, without the pressure of a workday." Zane set his pizza crust on the plate and gave her a serious look. "That's all right, isn't it?"

"Yes, it's fine. I can't thank you enough. I was just about to stick something in the oven. That is, if I could find anything."

His relaxed tone soothed her nerves. It pleased her that he seemed to care about the farm and was taking it seriously. Though she understood the reason he gave—that he felt he owed it to John—she found it hard to accept that sort of concern, kindness. But Riley wanted to believe him. She couldn't help but like Zane.

"You're going to spoil me if you keep this up. First the mechanic, then the laptop, and now pizza! What next?"

The spark in his eyes sent a thrill through her. To avoid his gaze, she wet a cloth at the kitchen sink then began wiping Chad off in his high chair, though she mused that hosing him down might be a better choice.

"Riley?" Her stomach swirled at the way he said her name. She closed her eyes. She needed to rein in her emotions now if she was going to make it through this evening.

He continued even though she hadn't answered him. "If it would make you feel more comfortable, you and Chad could freshen up while I clean up the dishes. Besides, your grandfather hasn't eaten. I can visit with him while I wait."

The man thought of everything. Though Riley loved his considerate nature, her grandmother's words flitted through her mind. *If it seems too good to be true, it probably is.* She thrust the negative thought away and turned to face Zane.

Grandpa whistled as he strolled through the living room and into the kitchen. "I smell pizza." His eyes widened, and he smiled with pleasure as he stuck out his hand to Zane. "Well, what do you know? Did you bring those pizzas? You might give my Riley some competition if you're not careful."

Riley smiled at her grandfather's teasing reference to her cooking, or lack thereof, and offered him a plate of the Italian food. "Grandpa, I need to get cleaned up and so does Chad. You don't mind visiting with Zane while I do that, do you?"

"Not at all. He's a fine young man."

Riley pulled an unwilling Chad out of his chair. "Come on, sweetie, don't you want to take a bath?" She headed up the stairs, trying to decide how to keep her eye on him while she cleaned up.

Zane's unexpected appearance was a pleasant surprise. But

she reminded herself that she wasn't exactly the best judge of character. She'd spent over a year with a self-centered control freak, all the while thinking he was her dream come true. Riley groaned. Zane's interest was a business one, connected to her brother, and she shouldn't allow her thoughts to venture anywhere else.

She entered the bathroom with Chad, turned on the water to ready his bath, and grinned. *At least until I get to know him better.*

❧

Riley descended the stairs into the living room. After his bath, she'd given Chad to the men to watch while she washed up. Grandpa lounged in his recliner watching a game show, his eyelids drooping. He'd probably retire to his room soon. Zane sat on the sofa, a sleeping Chad leaning against his arm. He smiled as she approached but appeared tense. She wasn't sure if he was afraid of waking Chad or if she'd taken too long to get ready.

"I'm sorry. I didn't mean to make you wait." Riley paused in the center of the room, looking at the occupied recliner and sofa. The only place left to sit was next to Zane. "You really don't have to stay."

Zane furrowed his brows and stared at her as if trying to read her meaning. "I don't want to keep you from doing anything."

"No, it's all right. We can talk about the farm. Right, Grandpa?" she asked.

In response, her grandfather rose from his exhausted stupor. He turned to grasp Zane's hand and shake it. "It was nice chatting with you, son. I've got an early morning, and it's my bedtime."

They bade Grandpa good night. Riley hoped they wouldn't

wake the sleeping boy. She sat in the warm chair her grandfather had vacated but noticed it wasn't positioned in a way
conducive to conversation. "Why don't we go to the kitchen
table? I can make us coffee."

"What about him?" Zane tilted his head toward Chad.

"I'll put him to bed." Riley carefully peeled Chad away from
Zane, tiptoed up the stairs, and placed him in his bed.

By the time she returned to the kitchen, the aroma of fresh-
brewed coffee wafted through the air. "You can't help yourself,
can you?"

Zane looked up from pouring the brew into a mug. "What?
Should I just wait for you to do everything?"

She warmed at his thoughtfulness. Still, for some reason, it
frustrated her. "No, but you could at least let me do something.
I read that when they designed instant cake mix they decided
to leave in a few steps, like adding eggs and water, so that the
homemaker would feel useful."

He laughed. "Okay, so I'll let you make the coffee next
time."

Next time?

He handed her the I LOVE CALIFORNIA cup, steaming with
black liquid. "I assume this is yours." He grinned. "Sorry, I
don't know what you take, so you'll at least have to do that
yourself."

"Give me that." She reached for the nondairy creamer and
dumped a spoonful in.

He shook his head. "I can't do this." He smirked before
continuing. "I can't let you go on with the wrong impression
about me—again. Your grandfather made the coffee while
you were cleaning up earlier. Said he liked the instant but
that you were 'dead set on your fancy brew,' to put it in his
exact words. All I had to do was walk in here and push the

button to start it."

"Well, now, that makes me feel better." She sipped the hot drink while questions about the man standing in her kitchen reeled in her mind. "So why don't you tell me about yourself. In only two days, you've turned yourself into a necessity at Sanderford Cranberry Farms, but I don't know a thing about you except that you were John's business partner."

Zane took a long drink of his coffee. Riley wondered how he could swallow it when it was piping hot. "Me? There's nothing too interesting about me. But maybe you'd like to talk about your brother. I know that you two only learned of each other a couple of years ago. And with you living across the country, you probably didn't get much time with him or his family." He moved to the kitchen table. "You would like to talk about him, wouldn't you?"

The pain she felt over her brother's death had become far too familiar. And she hated it. She swallowed the lump that formed in her throat and joined Zane at the table. "Yes. You're right. I would. So tell me, how did you two meet?"

"John and I have known each other since grade school. I wouldn't say we were friends, though, until high school, when I was going through some. . .things. We became close. He was like a brother to me. We attended different colleges. Public for him, private for me. But we stayed in touch. I knew him to be brilliant, and when I decided to start Cyphorensic, I discussed everything with John. He left a good job with great company benefits to join me."

As he spoke, Riley watched his handsome face contort. Lines she hadn't seen before appeared out of nowhere, making him look older than before.

He paused and scrutinized the knots in the pine table. "I can't tell you how sorry I am for your loss. That's why I want you to believe me when I say that I really want to make your farm a success."

His need for her approval took her by surprise. A myriad of emotions swelled inside, creating nervous flutters in her stomach, and she searched for a way to dispel them. "Would you like more coffee?"

She retrieved the carafe from the counter and set it on the table between her and Zane, like a protective barrier—though she wasn't quite certain what she needed protection from.

"No, thanks." He toyed with his empty cup, waiting for her response.

"Zane, I believe you. I know this has been quite a blow to you, too, not only in terms of losing a friend, but to your business, as well." Riley cleared her throat, trying to recover from the shakiness she heard there. "Have you hired John's replacement?" It was painful to speak of her brother. She was grateful for the coffee and took a big swig.

Zane rose from the chair and jammed a hand into his jeans pocket. He paced across the linoleum floor while he rubbed his chin. Riley had noticed that he often took time to consider things before he spoke. She liked that about him.

"I haven't been able to go forward, for reasons I can't explain right now." He stared at her as he sat down, leaning over the table to look intently into her eyes. "When was the last time you actually spoke to John? I mean, did you have a chance to talk to him before he died?"

Riley sighed. "Thankfully, yes. We only spoke every few weeks or so. If he didn't call me, I'd call him. Sometimes I'd talk to Sarah or Chad."

Zane frowned, and his expression took on that deep, contemplative look she'd become accustomed to, though it was usually interspersed with smiles. She reminded herself that the discussion of John was painful for him, as well.

"What about the night he died? Did you talk to him then?" Zane's gaze was penetrating, his expression serious.

"No. He'd called that night. But I didn't talk to him."

"Then how do you know he called? He left you a message?" Zane leaned forward. "What did he say?"

"I don't know if he left a message because I mistakenly deleted them. I know he called because I saw his number on my caller ID. I tried to return his call. Got no answer, so I left a message."

Zane's shoulders sagged. "What time was it when you checked messages—do you remember?"

Something in his tone sent prickles over her. He sounded like a cheesy detective questioning a suspect on a prime-time police drama. She rubbed her arms to take away the unexpected chill.

Unnerved by the conversation, Riley stood up. "Can you tell me why you want to know?"

He stiffened. "I'm sorry. I didn't mean to upset you."

"I know. It's just me. I'm tired, and talking about John, well, it's just too painful right now, I suppose. Look, could we do this another time? I mean, I want to talk more. I'd love to hear stories of my brother, since you knew him far longer than me." She smiled at him, hoping to ease the tension.

His expression relaxed, and he smiled gently. "Riley, truly. . .I didn't mean to overstep. But you're right. It's getting late, and I have an early day tomorrow. I need to get on top of all that paperwork." He flashed her another smile.

After Zane left, Riley locked the doors. She climbed the stairs and peeked in on Chad. Still sleeping. She wanted nothing more than to plop down on her bed, but she noticed a pile of envelopes on the pillow. Grandpa had placed her mail there instead of putting it in the office. Probably afraid her junk mail would get lost. She laughed and rummaged through the stash, some of which was forwarded from her California address, then tossed the mail into a cardboard box to be dealt with later. She still needed to unpack.

As she readied herself for bed, she couldn't stop thinking about Zane Baldwyn. She didn't doubt that his intentions to assist her with growing the farm were sincere. But his questions had sent a suspicious chill up her spine. She chided herself for revisiting the ridiculous notion. She'd probably misunderstood his intent and had overreacted. It wasn't as if she hadn't been emotional of late. Still, the niggling thought that he was after something wouldn't leave until she drifted off to sleep.

Riley woke with a start and sat up, her heart racing. Sweat beaded on her brow. The images came rushing back. She'd dreamed she was married to Eric. He was the absolute worst husband, thoughtless, inconsiderate. He traveled constantly and never had time for her, just like her father. Riley lay her head back against the pillow and let out a soft cry. In the dream, Eric's face had morphed into Zane's.

eight

Stupid! Stupid!

Zane slammed the door to his condo behind him. His car keys jingled when he tossed them onto the coffee table. The place smelled stale, neglected.

If it had been physically possible to kick himself, he would have. Instead, he settled for berating. He'd handled it all wrong, bungling his attempt to question Riley without raising her defenses or alerting her to his predicament. If he could solve this mess without involving her, it would be for the best. The last thing he wanted to do to John's grieving sister was create fear. Nor did he think it would do any good for her to discover her brother had been murdered. Zane could prove none of it. Yet.

It was a delicate balance—convincing her of his sincere attempt to help Sanderford Cranberry Farms while using the opportunity to sleuth. If he had learned anything about Riley O'Hare, it was that she had a few trust issues.

Slipshod, Baldwyn, truly slipshod.

The bottom line was that he didn't know how to question her and should have waited for a more suitable opportunity. He'd pushed things. So far, he'd gone about winning her confidence all wrong. He'd suspected that she didn't trust him from the beginning, so he'd labored to win her favor.

He thought he'd gained ground as he watched her warm smile, enjoyed their banter. But it was she who'd disarmed him and won his esteem. He laughed at the irony and headed for the shower.

Despite his best efforts, he'd only succeeded in ruffling Riley's feathers with his assistance, rather than pleasing her, right down to making coffee. Her first reaction to almost everything he did for her was to take it as a personal affront to her abilities. He was trying too hard.

He showered and dressed, then fell into a plush chair in the corner of his home office. Cardboard boxes from Cyphorensic were stacked and organized along the far wall, beckoning him. He ran his fingers through his still-wet hair and wondered why he'd dressed instead of getting into bed. Might as well get to work. He skimmed through papers in one of the boxes. Then another. When he looked up at the atomic clock, it read 1:00 a.m.

If he had done too much damage with his questions, Riley might not allow him back into the office, into her life. He couldn't risk it. He grabbed his keys and rushed out the door to head back to the Sanderford Cranberry Farms office. He should retrieve as much information as he could from the dinosaur computer and finish organizing the endless piles of papers. It would be pleasant to walk into a thoroughly scrubbed and orderly office tomorrow, as well.

Until Zane figured out what was going on, he would not let any questionable activities rest. While talking with Robert Sanderford tonight, he'd learned that Sarah had used the office computer. If she'd used it for even thirty seconds, she might have hidden information that would help Zane—if that had been John's plan. There was no way for him to know for sure whether Sarah had been involved unless he copied and examined the files on the computer.

In the meantime, he could possibly get an overview of Sanderford Cranberry Farms by looking at the files, depending, of course, on whether anyone had bothered to update things.

After the drive from Plymouth to Carver, Zane turned onto Cranberry Highway. Before long, he pulled into the entrance to Sanderford Cranberry Farms and turned off his headlights as he headed toward the office. He didn't want to disturb anyone. As the tires of his car crunched against the gravel driveway, they seemed to shout his presence, and he winced, hoping no one heard.

Rather than slamming his car door, he pressed it shut until he heard the required click. He crept up the steps to the office and searched through his key ring for the one Riley had given him earlier in the day.

One of the keys engaged the lock, and Zane exhaled. The thick smog polluting his mind suddenly cleared. He hadn't known what he was looking for until that moment.

The key!

He shut the door behind him and leaned against it, allowing the exhilarated pounding of his heart to calm. Why hadn't he thought of it before? The criminals who'd stolen the Cyphorensic computers needed the key to the encryption code, or the software would be of no use to them. Still, it didn't make sense. John was developing software to create a new encryption standard, but it wasn't finished. Why steal it? Though he didn't understand everything, Zane had at least figured out what John had hidden away somewhere, and his strong suspicion was that John had mailed the key to Riley. Only she would not recognize it for what it was.

In the dark, he stumbled to the desk and flipped on the banker's lamp, hoping the low lighting would be sufficient for him to see while he copied files. While he waited for the old computer to boot up, he spotted one of the scripture pictures that Riley had hung on the wall. The dim light on the desk wasn't bright enough for him to make out the words, so he strolled over.

He read it in a hushed tone. " 'Seek the Lord while he may be found; call on him while he is near.' Isaiah 55:6."

A sense of peace settled upon him, unnerving him. He backed away from the image. First Chelsea had said she would pray for him. Now his path had crossed with Riley, another Christian. She believed that it was her obligation to evangelize everyone, or at least she'd been upset with herself for not asking John if he had known Christ. It surprised Zane that she hadn't asked him yet, and he wondered what he would tell her if she did.

Sure, he was a Christian.

He believed in God and His Son. He'd learned all of that as a child. But he wasn't so sure that God cared much about the everyday details of his life. God hadn't exactly been there for him when things had fallen apart in high school. But John had. And Zane had picked up the pieces and made a success of his life.

He shook his head. Some success. His partner and wife were dead, and more than Zane's company was now at risk. The idea that God was trying to reach him for some reason wouldn't let go. Did God do that? Zane wasn't sure, but there was no way that he would believe God had gotten rid of John just to get Zane's attention. No. If he'd learned anything in Sunday school, it was that the human race lived in a fallen world. God wouldn't do something bad to achieve something good. Zane nodded to himself. Instead, He would act like any good manager and take something that had gone horribly wrong and create something good from it.

That was all Zane was trying to do here—solve a mystery to bring order back. Still, he wondered why God hadn't involved Himself in Zane's family crisis when he was in high school.

His ulcer flared, and he went back to the desk to find the bottle of antacid he'd stuck in the top drawer. He popped two of the pills and swallowed them dry; then he stuck a disk into the computer's drive and began the laborious task of copying files.

This would take awhile.

In the meantime, he opened drawers and pulled out all the items, organizing them while he waited. For all he knew, Riley had received the item John had sent and simply stuck it in a drawer, not realizing its importance. Nothing he did could be counted as a waste of time.

He smiled to himself. Though Riley could blame most of the disorganization on her grandfather, Zane had seen her in action and was convinced she'd learned all she knew from Robert. John was her half brother, but they were complete opposites. John was a well-oiled programming machine with a brilliant mind that seemed to border on insanity at times. He could not exist if anything was out of place. Riley seemed to thrive amid disorganization.

As he thought of Riley, warmth spread through his chest. In only a matter of a few days, he'd begun to care about her as more than John's sister. It sickened him to think of her reaction once she learned of the initial reasons for his proposal to help the cranberry farm. She would be angry and disillusioned. She'd lose faith in him. He was a fool to allow himself any attachment to her.

Zane shrugged off the nagging thoughts and focused on the task at hand. He filed every loose paper in its own category in manila folders, trashed others, and organized the boxes based on the dated information to be dealt with later. He swept the floor and shined the windows as well as possible in the darkened room. All the while, he continued to insert disks into the computer and copy the files. He was amazed at the amount of information on the machine, since it didn't sound as though Robert Sanderford had spent much time on it. Though he could have searched the computer itself without copying the files, he didn't want to take a chance that he would need access to the information again and for some reason that access would be denied. Riley might decide she didn't want his help anymore.

By three in the morning, he'd finished copying the last of the files and uncluttered the office of most of the excess papers. He would head home and attempt to get a few hours of sleep. Tomorrow morning he would return to the farm, then spend his evenings searching for John's key.

He thought of Chad, Riley, and Grandpa and prayed to God for the first time in years. He had to find the key to decipher John's code.

Before someone else did.

nine

After a difficult night of tossing and turning, Riley woke early and joined Grandpa for breakfast. She noted he was running behind this morning. She spoon-fed oatmeal to Chad to be sure that he ate something, because half of the mixture had already ended up on the floor. Grandpa slurped his instant coffee while he read the morning paper. She cleaned up the breakfast dishes and continued to peek out the window, eager for Zane to arrive.

"What's eating you this morning, Riley?" Grandpa tilted his head enough to peer at the paper through his bifocals.

She pulled up a chair and sat down at the table. Chad sipped the last of the milk. "Am I that obvious?"

"You've had four cups of coffee already and are brewing more. You've looked out the kitchen window between every spoonful of oatmeal and every dish you put away."

"I thought you were reading the paper," she teased. It probably didn't take much effort for him to see that she was about to burst. "I didn't sleep well last night. I'm just anxious to get things moving for you. That's all."

Anxious to throttle Zane is more like it!

She had awakened in the night after a bad dream and slipped out of bed to head to the kitchen for warm milk but remembered she had to save the last of the milk for Chad. When she'd looked out her bedroom window, she'd seen a light on in the office and Zane's parked car. By the time she'd slipped on her robe and hurried down the stairs, he'd gone.

She couldn't imagine what he would be after in the middle of the night. Had he left something? Nothing could be that important.

More than anything, she wanted to believe the best about him. She liked him. But his questions to her about John had seemed more like fishing than curiosity. She'd been tired and emotional about the discussion of her brother and had dismissed the nagging in the back of her mind that Zane wasn't being up front with her—that he was hiding something.

She wished she didn't jump to the worst conclusions about people, but her time with Eric had left her unable to trust. He'd told her he cared for her, and at first, it seemed that he did. But over time, Riley came to realize that only work mattered to him. Eric had used her, allowing her to take the blame for a disgruntled client when, in fact, the blame was all his.

Seeing Zane in the office at three in the morning had aroused her questions about his motives once again. For some reason, she felt betrayed. Used again. Nausea rolled through her stomach at her disappointment. She would confront him as soon as he arrived. Grandpa's chair scraped across the floor as he scooted from the table. The sound jolted Riley back into the present.

"Well, I'm off. Zane and I had a good talk last night. I need to check all our equipment to see what else needs to be repaired or replaced."

Riley's heart jumped. "Grandpa, I need to speak with Zane first when he gets here. Alone. Would you mind watching Chad for me for a few minutes while I do that? Then I'll take him to the grocery store with me. I can't put that off any longer. We'll have something home cooked for dinner tonight,

I promise." She hoped it wasn't an empty promise.

"Sure I can play with Chad while you take care of your business. I think I hear Zane's car now."

Riley placed a hand over her stomach as if it could quiet the turmoil inside. "Let me wipe Chad off first." She wetted a paper towel and cleaned his face, hands, and high chair. She needed to calm down before she went into the office. If anything, she'd need her mind to be clear before confronting Zane and his smooth talk.

The door stuck as she tried to plow through, bruising her arm and shoulder. She hurried across the circular drive between the house and the small office, then thrust the door open to confront Zane.

He stood behind the desk, opening the new laptop. When he saw Riley, he smiled and held out his arms as if showing off the fruit of his labor. "For you."

As she scanned the small room, she was speechless. The entire office appeared clean, swept, and polished. Even the outdoors appeared brighter through the sparkling windows. Though the cardboard boxes remained, they'd been re-positioned in an out-of-the-way part of the room. Each corner of each box appeared perfectly aligned. The desktop held no scattered, waiting-to-be-filed papers.

Her mouth dropped open.

"It's—it's truly amazing." Riley placed both of her hands on her head, scrunching her hair between her fingers. Relief swept though her in the form of sheer pleasure. "So this is why you were here in the middle of the night?" She frowned, remembering she'd been quick to judge him.

"I couldn't sleep. And, well. . .please don't take this wrong, but I couldn't stand the thought of facing this disorganized office another day. Now we're good to go. I wanted to research for the business plan today, but something else has come up." He looked down at the keyboard and began typing while he stood.

She strolled to the desk, disappointed. "You're leaving? You just got here." Embarrassment flooded her at her words. She'd sounded too needy. "I understand, though. You probably have plenty of other things to do." She hoped she was wrong.

"I'm not leaving—just have to take care of a few other things first."

An image of Chad and Grandpa flashed across her mind. "I almost forgot, I left Chad with Grandpa for a few minutes. He said he had things to do, so I don't want to leave him too long. I've got to go."

Zane stared intently at the computer screen without responding. Riley wasn't sure if he was listening as she said, "I want to be involved in everything to do with the farm, but I really need to go grocery shopping. So I hope there's nothing you need me for this morning."

She crept backward, figuring his mind was focused on something other than her.

Without looking up from the computer screen, he said, "Wait up. I'll go with you."

Flabbergasted, Riley hesitated before responding. "You're going grocery shopping with me? What on earth for?"

He closed the laptop and rounded the desk. "Actually, I need to get some sort of work clothes. I thought we could do that, too."

His words continued to stun her. "Farm work clothes?"

"That's right. Remember I said I was willing to get my hands dirty? Well, I can't do that in these clothes." He motioned to his green polo shirt and pale slacks. "Isn't there a farm supply store where I can purchase the appropriate clothing?"

"Like a pair of overalls and a plaid shirt?" Riley smiled at him and nodded. He continued to surprise her, thrill her. "Sure, come on. We'll go to Carver Farm and Pet Supply. Grandpa has always gotten his work clothes there. I used to love to go there with him as a child. It's a great place to chat with the locals, too."

&

Riley and Zane pulled into Sanderford Cranberry Farms after several hours of running errands. She unbuckled Chad from his car seat and detached it from Zane's vehicle while he opened the trunk and removed plastic grocery bags. The items he'd purchased today would allow him to work in the field without concern. She smirked at the thought, thinking she would believe it when she saw it. Zane was the ultimate professional, and he looked the part. Yet she couldn't believe how rugged and handsome he appeared after he'd changed into his work boots and jeans.

By the time she'd ushered Chad to the doorstep, Zane was back outside for more of the groceries. He stared into the distance toward the cranberry fields as he strolled to the car. She laughed at his eagerness to work with his hands. When everything had been unloaded, Zane hurried back to the office and Riley worked to tidy the kitchen.

Just as she finished putting away the groceries, Zane rushed in and grabbed her arm. "Come on. I want to show you something."

The excitement on his face made her curious, but Chad's eyes were drooping. She gave him a regretful frown and said, "I'm sorry, but it's going to have to wait. The little guy needs a nap."

"No, you can bring him, too. Put him in the stroller." The man was as giddy as a child.

Riley strapped a sleepy Chad into the jogger, and they headed toward the cranberry beds. When they cleared the two large maples that hid their view of the crop, Riley saw her grandfather's dozer pull to a halt in one of the new beds. She gasped and covered her mouth.

"They brought it this morning while we were shopping. See, that's your grandfather working the thing. I told him not to mention we expected it today so that it would be a surprise."

In her excitement, Riley started running with the jogger. Zane kept up with her though he wore new work boots. Gravel crunched behind them, and they skirted the road to allow a truck pulling a trailer heaped with loam to pass.

"Zane, I don't know what to say to you. How?"

His grin spread from ear to ear. "I made phone calls on my cell on the drive to and from the farm. It's amazing how much work you can get done that way. I scheduled for the loam to be delivered—after the dozer, of course."

"No, I mean—and don't take this wrong—but what about the money?"

Zane stopped Riley and turned her to face him. He stuck his hands into his pockets and stared at something in the distance. "Because I'm no longer paying your brother a salary, I'm funneling it into the farm instead. I'll work it out on paper. I know this is what he would have wanted."

Riley swallowed the lump emerging in her throat, uncertain about Zane's decision to put his money into the farm.

His expression became serious, his eyes penetrating as he looked at her. "Don't worry about me, Riley. I have income from other investments, and I'd set aside money for my enterprise with John. Cranberry farming is a minor detour. You can consider me a venture capitalist, if you want—I'm investing in Sanderford Cranberry Farms."

She nodded her acceptance. When they made it to the newly dozed bed, Grandpa climbed out of the huge machinery, smiling bigger than she'd seen him since she moved here.

❧

For the next several weeks, Zane labored with Riley and her grandfather on the cranberry farm, preparing the new beds while caring for the established crop. They finished by adding a layer of peat and topping it with six inches of sand. Cranberry vine cuttings were spread then plowed into the soil with a harrow. The newly planted beds were then irrigated. By the end of July, all that remained to do until the harvest was to weed, mow the dikes, and watch for pests.

It was laborious, but Zane had never been happier in his entire life. Working with his hands had a therapeutic effect on his body, ridding him of stress. Though he'd planned to create a business plan for the farm, he and Riley decided that, given the fact the growing season was upon them, it was more effective and morale boosting for everyone, especially her grandfather, to see progress through planting new beds. There would be plenty of time once that was done to work on expanding even more, maybe diversifying into other crops. Robert Sanderford had plenty of acreage for that.

Zane worked the farm during the day, spending any extra time with Riley and Chad, then devoted his evenings to going over the computer programs and files, looking for a clue that would point him to the decryption key—the only thing that could decode John's encryption algorithm. Though the police had apprehended the electronics thieves, Zane's computers were not in the hoard of stolen property, and the case remained open. Since they had exhausted all leads, the investigation had stalled. And still, the mystery surrounding John's death remained.

❧

As the end of September neared and the time to harvest

the cranberries grew closer, Zane walked across the dike, watching the sprinklers jet water over the growing plants, and he couldn't help but think about his budding relationship with Riley. He connected with her in a way he couldn't explain. Her inner strength drew him. Her sense of humor helped him to laugh at himself.

Since he'd arrived to help at the farm, he'd watched new growth appear on the vines, elongating the stems covered in leaves. Eventually, pink and white flowers had given way to tiny green pinheads. Now as he scanned the beds overflowing with the ripened berries, he hoped that his blossoming relationship with Riley would also bear fruit.

But he'd kept something hidden from her. The heaviness pressed down on him, drowning him in a bog of guilt. He shook his head. If he wanted to build a lasting relationship, he'd have to construct it on a strong foundation. He needed to tell her the truth.

A gusty breeze bathed him with water droplets from a nearby sprinkler, and he took a deep, calming breath. Somehow the fresh air and sunshine made all his problems seem smaller, less pressing. His mind was clearer, more astute now than it had ever been. What did he really know anyway? John and his wife had died in a car accident. Someone had stolen his computers. Could the two incidents be unrelated? He could have only thought he saw someone lurking at the office and overreacted. He had nothing to go on and knew that if it weren't for the peace he felt working on the farm, he would have gone crazy with the effort of wondering if John's past had ensnared him once again, leading to his death. Zane could know nothing for certain until he found the key.

More than anything he wanted to move past his mistakes, his paranoia. He needed to tell Riley the truth. She'd placed more pictures with Bible verses on the walls of the office. Her faith was a strong and important part of her life, so he'd read the verses and thought about them. The latest one was his favorite. The scripture said there was a time for everything. He allowed the verse to linger in his mind. . . . *A time to plant and a time to harvest.* A few of the words resounded in his thoughts. . . . *A time to love and a time to hate.* He hoped for the former rather than the latter when he told her the truth.

"Zane!" Riley waved her arms from the road and sauntered toward him. As he watched her slim body maneuver the dikes with grace, he wondered if working on the farm had been the therapy, or if working with Riley was the real reason for his contentment.

He strolled toward her to meet her halfway. It was time to tell Riley the truth.

ten

Riley studied Zane as he headed toward her across the dike. It amazed her to see the transformation that had taken place in him over the last several weeks. He'd replaced his business suits with work jeans and shirts, but the change had penetrated deeper than just the clothes on his back.

As he approached with a gleaming smile that appeared to go to the depths of his soul, he tried to avoid one of the far-reaching sprinklers by running. He ended up thrusting his arms in a defensive posture as he passed the onslaught, getting sprayed anyway. His laughter resounded in her ears, making her heart skip. She licked her dry lips and reached for the ointment in her pocket.

Zane came to stand before her, stuck his hands in his pockets, and grinned down at her. "What's up?"

"Why don't you join us for dinner tonight? You always rush off. But how about some of my home cooking instead?" She stared at the ground, suddenly embarrassed. "I've been practicing and learning new recipes."

He laughed at her comment but didn't respond.

"You don't have to be afraid. Grandpa says I've improved. But I can see in his eyes that he misses my grandmother's cooking. He can't fool me there."

The light breeze whipped a strand of hair across her eyes. Zane reached over and pulled it out of her face then tucked it behind her ear. She gazed into his intense blue eyes and tried to hide from him how his simple touch had affected her.

"I'd love to join you, but..."

Though her grin remained in place, her disappointment sent a pang of regret through her. She licked her lips. "But?"

"I have a better idea. Let me rephrase that. Not better than eating your home-cooked food, I'm sure." He took her hand in his, causing her heart to race. "I have something important I need to talk to you about. I'd like to take you out to dinner. Alone. Maybe Grandpa could watch Chad for a while?" He raised his eyebrows.

Riley wondered when she would stop being surprised by anything Zane did. "Well, I still have to cook for my guys, but I suppose I could wait to eat with you." She paused while she considered her next question then asked, "Can you tell me what this is about? Have you finished the business plan? Or is it something else?"

"I'm researching before I put the document together, but that isn't what this is about." He furrowed his dark brows, his expression serious. "This is something else. You'll have to wait."

Riley wanted to question him further. She wondered if he had decided to stop working on the farm and simply put the business plan together at home. After all, he'd devoted much more time and effort to this place than she ever expected of him.

"Well then, I'll see you this evening. Is six all right? That will give me time to feed Chad and Grandpa then clean up the kitchen." She grimaced when she considered how tired she would be by then, but she looked forward to going to dinner with Zane.

"Six it is. I want to mow the far side of the dike; then I'll get showered and changed." He grinned and turned his back to her as he strolled toward the mower.

She shook her head. She never would have thought he would do this sort of work. And like it. Though he hadn't said it in so many words, she could see by the calm expression on his face and his relaxed posture that the farm had been good for him.

As she meandered next to the cranberry beds, hope swelled inside her that Grandpa's farm would eventually bring in more money. With Zane's help, they'd been able to make use of the planting season instead of putting it off for another year. Depending on what he came up with in his business plan, the next few years could mean big growth for Sanderford Cranberry Farms—if that was what her grandfather truly wanted.

Since John had considered Zane a worthy business partner, Riley measured the possibility of Zane staying connected to the farm in some way. Though he'd never indicated he would work with them from now on—he'd make a great consultant—she wanted him allied with them in a more permanent fashion. Still, Sanderford Cranberry Farms had been family owned and operated for ninety years, and she wasn't sure how Grandpa would feel about a partnership with Zane.

It saddened her to think that part of her grandfather's dream was not only to expand the farm, but to make it a family legacy for generations to come. With the rest of the family deserting the farm and going to take jobs in the city, no one was left to run it. Except Riley. She'd always treasured her time with her grandparents when she was growing up and loved the excitement of the harvest and the festival. But Riley and her mother had been whisked away by Riley's father to the other side of the country, all for the sake of his job.

Though her father remained consumed with his business

in California, they'd spoken over the phone several times since her move, and he promised to come to the farm for Christmas.

The holidays. The familiar pain over John's death surrounded her heart as she yanked the back door open and went into the kitchen. She decided to bake a one-dish recipe for easy cleanup rather than the five-course meal she'd planned to impress Zane with, giving herself more time to prepare for the date.

She pulled out a baking dish. He hadn't said it was a date, only that he needed to speak with her, that it was important.

Elsie entered the kitchen. "Hi, Riley. Chad's asleep. Can I help with anything?"

Riley shook her head and placed some ground meat in the microwave to defrost it. "No, thanks anyway. If Chad's asleep, you can go home." The tall brunette teenager had been an answer to prayer. She was Millie's granddaughter and lived only a couple of farms down on Cranberry Highway. Riley suspected that Millie's original intent of offering Elsie as a babysitter was to give Millie an additional reason to speak to Riley's grandfather.

"Okay, I'll see you tomorrow after school, then." The fifteen-year-old grabbed her satchel and headed out the door to walk home.

After mixing together a casserole, Riley popped it into the oven and set the timer for an hour then headed upstairs to get ready while Chad slept. If things went as planned, she'd have time to spend reading her Bible. After checking in on Chad, still sleeping in his toddler bed, she took a shower.

She reminded herself that Zane had not said it was a date. But it was difficult to keep from getting excited about the prospect of spending time alone with him, discussing anything at all over dinner. She wondered why he couldn't tell her in the office. In fact, they'd been alone when she'd come to the cranberry beds to invite him to dinner.

She knew she shouldn't harbor hope that his invitation had been a date disguised as something else. Though her relationship with Eric was in the past, thoughts of him still haunted her at times—maybe because he'd tried so hard to keep his hold on her, refusing to accept their breakup. Sometimes she feared she would open the door and see Eric standing there. A crazy thought, she knew. At first, Zane's workaholic attitude had reminded her of Eric. But as Zane had mentioned a few times, she'd had the wrong impression about him.

And he was right. Zane was nothing like Eric. Zane appeared to care about people, considering how every action taken and every word spoken would affect them. Eric, on the other hand, was greedy and self-serving.

Now that she considered it, when she had learned about her half brother in Massachusetts, Eric hadn't expressed any interest in the situation until she'd told him how John was hoping to develop new hack-proof encryption software. She regretted that slip of her tongue, but in her excitement, she hadn't thought to keep secrets from her boyfriend. For all she knew, he'd shared the news with some of his high-level business contacts and the vultures had circled, wanting in on the cyber action.

But John never said a word.

Riley wrapped a towel around her wet hair and peeked in on Chad. He slept curled up in a ball in the corner of his bed. She hurried to the chair in her room and grabbed her Bible off the side table. Taking a deep, calming breath, she reminded herself that she'd come to the farm to find peace and have time with God, not to rush through everything or become stressed while she prepared for dinner with Zane.

She tried to clear her mind of distractions and focus her thoughts on the Lord, but she couldn't quit thinking about Zane. There was something she needed to discuss with him, too, and she might as well do it tonight. She'd been remiss in allowing herself to care about him. Zane had said he believed in God. But did believing in God make someone a Christian? Or was it trusting in God? She remained unconvinced about his commitment to the Lord, not because he'd declined on several occasions to attend church with her, but because he avoided any discussion about God. But then, Riley hadn't always been ready to discuss her relationship with God, either—something she should have freely shared. She frowned then prayed for God to make her stronger.

She turned to Matthew 10, where she'd left off reading. "I am sending you out like sheep among wolves. Therefore be as shrewd as snakes and as innocent as doves." The words pierced her heart with conviction. She thought again of Zane's comments to her. *"I don't want to give you the wrong impression."*

Riley considered everything she knew about Zane. Frankly, it wasn't much. As a person, he was kind and considerate, hardworking. Still, a niggling doubt in the back of her mind continued to bother her.

He'd put an unbelievable amount of time and effort into Sanderford Cranberry Farms, for John's sake, he said. She believed him. But she knew he'd neglected his own company, because every time she questioned him, he told her he'd put Cyphorensic aside for a while. But why? Clearly, there was much about him she didn't know. She had trouble buying the fact that an entrepreneur such as Zane would put anything, especially the company he'd started, on hold. She pushed the unwelcome thoughts away, because she appreciated and wanted Zane's help. Still, she had to guard her heart somehow. She didn't relish the thought of being hurt again.

A child's cry reached her from across the hall, and she rushed into Chad's room. She pulled him out of his bed and discovered his body was on fire with fever.

ந

As Zane readied himself for dinner with Riley, he tried to get his mind off the possible outcome. He wasn't sure how she would respond when he told her what he'd kept from her all this time. But because he finally believed the crisis had long gone and that he'd been wrong about everything, he hoped her reaction to the news would be a mild one. With that behind him, perhaps he could tell her he was interested in pursuing a relationship. He blew out his breath, anxiety burning in his gut. He'd never been good with women.

He needed to focus on going forward with Cyphorensic again. Because nothing had surfaced regarding his stolen computers, John's brainchild of new encryption software was gone. Zane had been unable to locate a copy of the software, which frustrated him. He couldn't imagine that John hadn't kept a copy somewhere. Zane had no choice but to return to his original vision for Cyphorensic as a computer forensics software provider.

Of course, there was still the possibility that the criminals who stole John's software would attempt to use it, but they'd have to break John's code first, which was unlikely. Though it had never been far from Zane's mind, he needed to begin the search for John's replacement. In truth, no one could replace John—either in terms of his brilliance or in terms of his friendship to Zane. But it was long past time to put the past behind him and return to his normal life.

When he finished showering, his cell phone vibrated on the dresser and he picked it up. Riley's number flashed across the display, and he clenched his jaw. He dialed into voice mail to retrieve the message, hoping their plans hadn't changed.

Riley's worried voice resounded through the small device, explaining that Chad suffered with a fever and she didn't feel comfortable leaving him. Zane returned her call, and Robert answered. He said that Riley had been in contact with a nurse and had given Chad a fever reducer. Zane snapped the cell shut, feeling both disappointed and concerned over Chad at the same time.

He ordered in Chinese, and after he finished eating, he reclined on the sofa and fell asleep.

Buzz. Buzz. Buzz.

The vibration stirred Zane from a deep slumber, and he fumbled for the phone in his pocket. He glanced at the clock as he flipped open the device, which displayed Riley's number. One thirty in the morning.

Apprehension coursed through his body. "Hello?"

"Zane! I've been trying to call you. Why haven't you answered? You won't believe what's happened."

The distress in Riley's voice urged him to the door. He grabbed his keys and left the condo. "Calm down, Riley. Is it Chad? Is he all right? Call the doctor." He climbed into his vehicle and spun out of the parking lot.

"No, Chad is fine. I gave him a fever reducer. It worked. It's the office—someone has ransacked our office."

eleven

Chad fell back to sleep while Riley clutched him, waiting for Zane to arrive. She felt guilty that she still held on to the child, but she wanted to know that he was safe and secure after what had happened. The police had already come and gone, which reassured her. She tiptoed up the stairs and laid him back on his bed.

After taking care of Chad, she returned to the kitchen and poured herself another cup of coffee, realizing that she wouldn't get any sleep tonight. Grandpa leaned against the counter with his cup, lost in thought. Though she'd tried to contact Zane before the authorities, he hadn't responded to her initial attempts to reach him. Now as she considered her actions, she wondered why he was the first person she'd thought to call.

She tried him again after the police had left. It had seemed surreal when the two cruisers raced up the cranberry farm drive. She'd answered a series of questions and was told to expect an officer from the Bureau of Crime Investigation to take photos and recover prints the next day.

Headlights flashed through the kitchen window. Riley and Grandpa headed out the door to greet Zane. He stepped out of his car, and without thinking about her actions, Riley flew into his arms. He held her tight as if it were the most natural thing to do. The warmth and security she felt within his muscled frame comforted her. When she became aware that she was clinging to Zane, she distanced herself.

"I'm. . .um. . .sorry about that. It's just that this whole mess. . ." She gestured toward the office and averted her gaze from his questioning eyes.

"No, no. It's all right."

Zane nodded to Grandpa. "Sorry you've had to go through this, Robert."

"It's not your fault, son." He placed his hand on Zane's shoulder and squeezed. "I'm just glad you finally got here to help calm Riley down."

Wide-eyed, Riley gazed at her grandfather. "What's that supposed to mean?"

"Come on. Let's go inside." Zane gave her a sympathetic smile and grabbed Riley's arm.

"You kids have fun. I'm heading back to bed." Disgruntled, Grandpa turned his back to them and walked to the house. "I'll listen for Chad. No need to worry."

"Can you tell me what happened?" He started toward the office.

She ran ahead and stood in front of the door. "No, we shouldn't go in here. Let's talk in the kitchen."

"We won't go in. But I want to see for myself."

"All right." Riley opened the door for him.

Brows furrowed, Zane stood in the doorway, his gaze roaming over the destruction. With a deep frown, he nodded at Riley. "I've seen enough. Now tell me what happened."

She descended the porch steps and walked with him to the house.

"I got up to check on Chad because of his fever. I saw lights on in the office again, and at first I thought it was you. So I dressed and came outside in time to see the vandals drive away."

He held the door for her as she entered.

"Did you see what kind of car they drove, their license plate?"

"It was too dark to read the license plate, but I saw a sedan. Not sure of the make. It looked like an expensive model, though. I've already told all of this to the police." Riley shuddered when she considered how close she'd come to walking in on them.

Zane pulled her to him, embracing her. "Are you cold?" He rubbed her arms to generate heat. But instead she felt the warmth rushing to her cheeks.

"No, I'm really not cold. Just shaken. Oh, Zane, the longer I stared at the papers strewn over the floor and the overturned boxes, the angrier I became. It's so. . .frustrating."

She pushed away from his attempt to console her. "I don't understand why anyone would do this. It makes no sense. And all the hard work you've done is for nothing. It's not like we have a problem with vandals out here. What do you think, Zane? Why would someone do this?"

His expression grim, he said, "I can't tell you how relieved I am that you didn't walk in on them. There's no telling what they might have done. In fact, don't come out here at night alone for any reason." He nailed her with a convicting stare. "What if something would have happened to you? What about Chad?"

"But I thought it was you." Her voice cracked with emotion.

He placed his hands on Riley's shoulders. "I'm sorry about that. About everything." He hung his head. The stress and tension she'd watched dissipate from him over the last several weeks were back in full force.

A sense of foreboding pressed against her thoughts. Zane's strange questions came to mind. *"Did you have a chance to talk to him before he died?"* All her doubts about his reasons for working on the farm whirled in her head, creating a tumultuous whirlpool of suspicion. But she'd put them to rest already and tried to dismiss them again.

"Grandpa said that no one has ever done this before. I'm thankful they were only interested in destroying the office and didn't venture to the house. I get the sense they were looking for something, but I can't imagine what. Can you?"

A shadow flashed across Zane's features. Riley's pulse raced. Her mind played tricks on her, persuading her to suspect that the vandalism was related to Zane and not to Sanderford Cranberry Farms.

"I don't want to give you the wrong impression." His earlier words danced in her mind, mocking her.

She turned her back to him and began rinsing out her coffee mug at the kitchen sink. "Do you think it was vandals, Zane, or do you think they were looking for something?" *And what?* She wanted to voice her last question but dreaded the answer; she could hardly breathe while she waited for his reply.

It never came.

Riley lifted her face and stared at the ceiling, taking a deep breath. She turned to face Zane, and what she saw in his eyes shredded all that was left of her hope.

❧

The look in Riley's eyes squeezed Zane's chest like a vise. He'd never meant for this to happen, for things to go this far. His mind reeled from the shock that Sanderford Farms had been targeted. Why had they waited until now? Zane rubbed his stubbled jaw.

He hastened to Riley, put his hands on her shoulders, and peered into her eyes. They shimmered with a mixture of hurt, anger, and distrust. "Remember when I asked you to believe me, to trust me, when I said that I was helping with the farm because I owe it to John—for your sake and Chad's?"

She nodded slowly.

A sharp pain shot through his chest at what he was about to tell her. "Riley, I think you need to sit down."

She snapped out of her stunned expression and pulled away. "No, tell me everything. Now." Her voice sounded distant, unfeeling.

He grabbed her, forcing her to face him. "I meant every word. In fact, it didn't take long for my desire to help you with the farm to become something I wanted to do for you, regardless of John."

Riley stumbled to the chair and slumped into it. "Tell me why you came to work here. The truth."

Zane ran both hands through his hair and blew out a breath. *Where do I begin?* "The night that John died, I heard him leave you a message." He cleared his throat. "The corridors in our office suite echo, and well. . .John hadn't closed his door. I mistakenly overheard him."

Riley quirked her left brow. "And?"

"I heard John say he'd sent something to you. Then as he hung up, he said it might be a matter of life and death. He sent something he considered to be very important to you, Riley."

Riley covered her face with her hands then let them drop to her lap. "What else?"

"It wasn't until after the funeral when I decided to look at John's laptop that I discovered it missing along with all of his hardware and storage devices. I just. . .couldn't bring myself to go into his office. Had to give myself time."

She pushed herself from the chair and moved to face him. "So what are you saying, exactly? I still don't understand why you came to work here." Her voice was riddled with emotion. "Unless you're looking for whatever the vandals were looking for here, too. That's it, isn't it?"

Her brows knitted in confusion, and her pain was evident in her frown.

With all of his being, Zane wanted to make her understand. "I never intended to use you. I only wanted to protect you. You have your hands full, and I wasn't sure about any of this anyway." Still, he kept the burden of John's possible murder to himself.

"Did they find it?" she asked.

He shrugged. "I don't know. Do you remember getting anything from John in the mail?"

"If you could tell me what we're talking about, that might help."

Riley's voice sounded steady, and she appeared more composed, more accepting of the circumstances. Despite the situation he'd placed her in, she remained resilient.

"My vision for Cyphorensic was to enter the growing computer forensics field." He glanced at Riley and noted a question in her eyes. "Computer forensics is used by investigators to determine if illegal activities have transpired on a computer system. I brought John on board, but because he'd already begun work on creating a new standard in encryption code—meaning hack-proof code—that's the direction we took. I can count on one hand the programs out there that are considered undecipherable. The government uses them."

His explanation complete, he shrugged. "That's where we're at. The only conclusion I can make is that whoever stole the computers must have wanted John's software. But they can't open it because John's work can't be hacked. Obviously, they're looking for the key to crack the code."

Riley shook her head. "Why would they think they could find it here? A password, for crying out loud."

"Not just any password. John would have created a complicated algorithm." What would Zane have done had he needed access to the software?

"Great, just great." Riley rubbed her arms.

"Hold on." Zane paced as he thought. Riley waited, seeming to understand his need for concentration. Then it dawned on him. "That's it."

"What's it?"

He gripped his chin. "They must have hired another hacker to break the code but were unsuccessful. It's the only explanation. Apparently, their tactic hasn't worked, and now they're searching again. They must think I've hidden it somewhere."

"Still, why don't they just confront you? Ask for it?"

"Hear me out. I've wondered why they haven't confronted me, too." Zane hesitated. He didn't want to reveal to Riley that he believed John had been murdered or had been involved in something illegal. "Maybe they hope they can find John's key by following me. If they were to confront me too soon, they might risk losing the key for good, now that John is gone."

Riley shook her head, her expression grave. "Zane, eventually, if they don't find this. . .password. . ."

"That's why we have to find it first."

"But I still don't know what we're looking for."

"What we're looking for is both simple and complicated. John enjoyed creating puzzles to solve, hidden treasures. John has hidden the key. He has left us the clue of where to find it. I'm sure of it."

"So what is the clue? The sooner we get this solved, the better." She thrust her hands on her hips, determined.

"Well, there's another problem. I don't even know what the clue is." He dispelled her wide-eyed expression with a wry grin. It relieved him to see her appear to have overcome the situation. Her strength amazed him.

More than anything, he wanted to pull her into his arms, but he steeled himself and instead raised his arms out to her as if making an offering. "I'm so, so sorry, Riley. I never meant for any of this to happen. I thought I would figure it out, that I could manage it on my own. I didn't want to give you something else to worry about."

She pressed her lips together and turned away then began wiping the kitchen counter. She stopped. Her actions indicated that she still held animosity toward him. He watched her reach into her jeans pocket and pull out a small tube, probably her lip ointment. A familiar, nervous act he'd seen her perform numerous times. When he considered all he'd come to know about her, down to her constant need to moisturize her lips, a sense of longing coursed through him.

"You'll have to bear with me, Zane. This has been information overload for me. Right now, I just don't know what to think. I do know we've got to find that clue. You should have told me this from the beginning."

Riley twisted her hair back and pinned it with a clip she'd pulled from a drawer. He watched her reflection in the glass of a picture hanging on the wall.

And then he knew where John had hidden the clue.

twelve

Zane unlocked the entrance to his condo, the events of the night reeling through his mind. He closed the door behind him, locked it, then shut his eyes and leaned back against the sturdy steel casing. The cold penetrated his clothing while he repeatedly knocked the back of his head against the door, furious with himself for allowing the situation to escalate.

He'd finally become convinced that he'd made a mistake—that the stolen computers were a simple matter of theft with no ties to John. But he could afford no such errors again. Come morning, he would hire his own private investigator.

He flipped the switch on the wall, but the sofa lamp did not yield its light.

Fear gripped his gut.

He stood motionless and listened, hoping he hadn't stumbled into trouble.

After his eyes adjusted to the moon's rays filtering through the blinds, he recognized the same chaos he'd witnessed at the Sanderford Farms office. Only the culprits had done much more damage to Zane's residence. His leather sofa had been upended, along with the lamp and side table. The chairs had fared no better.

He hoped the culprits wouldn't decide to return. Zane could not understand what good could come of scattering papers and overturning furniture in order to search for their treasure. If anything, he believed it would only make the hunt more difficult.

John had counted on his need for order to alert Zane to his clue. He clenched his jaw, gritting his teeth. The item had been before John the whole time, sitting on the desk in the open, when it should have been hanging on the wall out of his workspace. He was relentless to keep his desk tidy and free of anything that would distract him from his work, considering even a picture clutter. No one would have noticed an object out of place in John's logically arranged office. No one except Zane. Yet he had missed it.

It had been John's life insurance; of that, Zane felt confident. Somehow, John's plan had ended in disaster.

Zane had failed miserably, as well. He'd noticed the oddity, but because he hadn't realized he would need the information, he'd deleted the file from his mind. So it didn't register as anything but peculiar. He supposed the shock of the theft had skewed his ability to focus.

He picked his way through the living room over to the kitchen to flip on the fluorescents then crept down the empty corridor, remaining alert to any intruders, and into the office. He flicked the switch. Again nothing. The lamp in the office had also been overturned. Zane made a mental note to replace all of his lighting with overheads.

A bright ray of moonlight gleamed through the window, illuminating the one item he'd been searching for. He stepped softly, careful to avoid damaging any of the files or knick-knacks that lay scattered over the dark carpet. The image of Riley's look-alike stared up at him in the shimmering light like a shining specter in the dark room. Zane reached down to retrieve it. The picture appeared undamaged, but someone had stepped on it, cracking the glass and overlooking its significance.

He pulled the photo out and tossed the frame back into

the disaster area. The glass clinked as it hit the floor, but another slight jingle caught his attention. *Of course!* The clue was inside the frame. Zane recovered it and discovered a gold chain taped to the backing.

Bingo!

He dangled the chain in the moonlight. Still, he had no idea what it meant, only that it should lead him somewhere. Exhaustion overwhelmed him. He wanted to sit down but didn't have the energy to return the furniture to its proper position. There wasn't any point in calling the police, because he knew he wouldn't be giving them the evidence they would need to tie it all together—John's clue. He couldn't afford to lose the clue when he'd only just found it. Would they believe him anyway? Before heading to bed, he made sure to check all the closets and possible hiding places. He clutched the chain and the photo as he strolled to his bedroom, hoping he still had a bed to lie in.

It remained in its rightful place. Relieved and surprised at the same time, Zane plopped down on the soft mattress. He stared at the chain. Finding the clue was only the first piece of John's convoluted puzzle. He grimaced at the thought.

❧

Unwelcome sunlight flickered through the window as rustling leaves seemed to clatter outside, igniting Zane's headache. Groggily, he rolled out of bed and scowled at the disaster area that had been his home. The clock on the wall read eight thirty—he'd overslept. He headed for the bathroom and gaped at his coarse appearance. Shadows circled his eyes, and he needed a shave.

First, he would brew coffee to clear his mind. Last night he'd been too worn out to consider the events with clarity. But Riley had never left his thoughts. She'd lived in his dreams.

He'd hurt her by not being honest when he'd only tried to protect her, keep her from having another burden to add to her struggle. Now she had the trouble despite his efforts, and to make matters worse, he was afraid that she might erect a barrier between them. He had no idea if it could ever be torn down. He believed he'd made headway in earning her trust, but for what reason if it all came to this?

He splashed water over his face and dried it. Grabbing the chain and photo, he strolled to the kitchen, ignoring the untidy heap along the way. He laid the items on the counter and, after starting the coffee, decided to shower while it brewed. The photo drew his attention, and he stared at it. The woman held a cell phone to her ear and wore the same gold chain around her neck, but with a small locket affixed to it.

Riley must have the locket. That was what John had sent to her. Zane phoned her while he waited for the shower to steam.

No answer.

Thirty minutes later, Zane had dressed and was on his way down Cranberry Highway toward Sanderford Farms. He tried calling Riley but received no answer at the house. The day they'd gone shopping, she had purchased an answering machine, complaining about people who were hard to reach. He tried the farm office and left a message. It was reasonable to think that they were on the farm, especially with the imminent harvest.

Zane peeled through the entrance and down the gravel road. A luxury sedan that he didn't recognize was parked in the circular drive. He recalled Riley's words that the vandals had driven an expensive-looking sedan.

He tried to steady his breathing, but the events of the past evening would not allow him to do so. As soon as he stopped his vehicle, he exploded from it and dashed up the office steps to whip the door open. Empty.

He ran to the house, fueled by fear and adrenaline. Without knocking, he burst through the back door and, seeing the kitchen vacant, yelled Riley's name.

A dark-suited man stepped into the living area doorway, his eyes narrowed as he scrutinized Zane.

Oh no! Riley!

Rage pounded through his heart. In two steps, he stood before the stranger, fist drawn.

Riley appeared in the doorway. Her eyes widened, and she gasped. "Zane, no!" She stepped between him and the man.

Seeing her unharmed, he slumped against the wall, relieved. "Riley, you're all right."

He looked at the stranger standing next to her. The man wore a smirk on his face. Zane wanted to punch him anyway.

She placed her hand on his arm, its calming effect working. "Yes, I'm fine. Now what about you? You look like you've seen a creature from the latest horror flick."

"I thought. . . I thought. . ." He pushed away from the wall and paced, running his hands through his hair. "I'm sorry. I suppose after everything that has happened I thought the worst when I saw the unfamiliar car outside, and then I came in here to see him standing there. . . ."

She smiled in sympathy, yet she appeared tense and uncomfortable. Zane assumed she hadn't forgiven him for his duplicity.

Realization dawned in her eyes. "Oh, Zane, this is Eric Rutherford. Eric, Zane Baldwyn."

Zane nodded his acknowledgment, as did Eric, but neither shook hands.

Riley moved into the kitchen and sat down at the table.

"I'd prefer we talk in here; Chad's napping. Eric and I were. . . friends. . .when I lived in California. His arrival is an unexpected surprise." Eric pulled out the chair next to Riley and sat, placing his hand on hers. He laughed as his gaze slithered to Zane and back to Riley. "Come now, Riley. You know we were more than friends. Be honest with Zane." He kissed her hand.

Riley pulled her hand away, her face ashen.

Pangs of jealousy sliced through Zane's exposed heart. "I called but couldn't reach you."

"You did? That's funny. I didn't hear it ring, and I don't see the little red light flashing." She pushed away from the table and strode to the machine on the counter.

"There was no answer," Zane said, never taking his eyes from Eric. He didn't like the man.

Riley pushed buttons on the device. "Strange. It seems to be working."

Eric stood, as well, and buttoned his black suit coat. Zane cringed, wishing he'd dressed professionally today. Feeling humiliated already after his wrong assumptions, it would go a long way toward giving him a sense of authority.

"You were putting Chad down for a nap. I unplugged the phone, thinking you wouldn't want the boy disturbed." Eric came to stand behind Riley and placed his hands on her shoulders.

She turned to face him, looking like a cornered animal. "Zane, why were you trying to reach me?"

"It can wait." Zane didn't know how much he could say in front of Eric. "I've got things to do. It was nice to meet you, Eric."

Zane turned and left the house, wishing there was something he could do to extract Riley from Eric's possessiveness. But he had no right to act out of jealousy. No right to interfere.

❧

Grandpa appeared in the doorway. "Who's your friend, Riley?"

Thankful for Grandpa's arrival, she escaped Eric's assertive overtures and grabbed her grandfather's arm. "Grandpa, this is Eric Rutherford. He's a friend from California."

The older man thrust out his hand in his usual warm manner. "Glad to meet you, son. So you knew my Riley in California?" While keeping his attention on Eric, he ambled to the sink to fill a glass with water.

"Yes, we were close. I'm surprised she didn't mention me. So sorry to hear about her brother. Since I had business in Boston, I took the opportunity to stop for a visit. In fact, I'm taking a few extra days after my business is complete."

Riley closed her eyes. Nausea gripped her already-tumultuous insides, and her spirits sank. *No, no, no.*

Eric was the last person on the planet she wanted to see right now, if ever.

She needed to speak to Zane, unload her torrential emotions. *Go home, Eric.*

Given that Zane had tried to contact her and leave a message, she considered that he'd possibly discovered something to help them solve this ridiculous puzzle. She glared at Eric for his interference and would have growled at him if her trusting grandfather were not in the room.

Grandpa spoke to Eric about the plans for the farm and Riley's part in it, bragging on her. Riley felt the heat warm her cheeks, but her embarrassment stemmed from the fact that it had been Zane who'd gotten things rolling, not her. Her heart skipped at the thought of seeing him preparing to slug Eric. He'd tried to save her from someone he thought was a danger to her. She wished she hadn't stopped him.

Zane had appeared crestfallen when Eric took her hand.

It hurt her to see him like that. She'd have to explain Eric's presence once she had a chance to speak to him.

Both Grandpa and Eric stared at her, waiting for a response. "I'm sorry. Were you talking to me?"

"I just told Eric that he's welcome to stay here on the farm when his business is finished. We've got plenty of room, and that way he won't have to drive back and forth to see you."

The room tilted, and Riley leaned against the counter. She remained stunned for a moment while she contemplated a response. Grandpa had already made the offer; he didn't understand Riley's animosity, and she didn't want to seem rude to either of them. At least she would have time to come up with an excuse before Eric's minivacation.

"That's very kind of you, Grandpa. Thanks for coming by, Eric." Hearing Chad's cry, she jumped at the chance to leave. "I've got to check on Chad."

It was a struggle to contain her irritation with Eric, but it was best not to offend him, especially in front of her grandfather. He wouldn't understand her rudeness and would be disappointed in her.

When she reached Chad's room, she wiped away his tears and pulled him to her. After changing his diaper, she took him to her room to play on the floor while she tried to pray. She looked out her window toward the Sanderford Farms office.

Zane's vehicle was gone.

thirteen

A zesty autumn breeze wafted over Riley as she strolled near the cranberry beds. After the police had dusted for prints and completed their investigation, she'd spent the rest of the morning cleaning up the office. Alone. Eric had gone back to Boston to work, and Zane had never returned. Elsie had stopped by the farm after a short school day and offered to stay with Chad—an answer to Riley's prayer for help today. More than anything, she needed to calm her frazzled nerves. Last night's break-in and Eric's arrival this morning had almost brought her to her knees, as well it should. She needed to spend time in prayer. But she couldn't.

She bristled in irritation that she'd been kept from speaking with Zane. He had something to tell her. She knew because he'd all but said it when he mentioned that he'd tried to call her. She could see in his eyes that he wanted to talk to her alone. But he'd left the farm. She cringed when she thought of his hurt expression when Eric had acted as though she belonged to him.

Last night she'd learned that Zane had not been truthful about working at the farm. At first, the knowledge of his deception had hurt. The pain had gone deeper and felt more personal than it should have, surprising her. But she'd had time to consider his reasons and understand them. For now, she intended to focus on searching with Zane for whatever John had hidden.

Still, she wondered what else he kept from her. She believed in Zane, but a certain part of her remained unwilling to trust him completely.

The brilliant crimson fruit helped to calm her spirit, and as she stared down at the beds, she decided the ripened crop did, indeed, deserve the name *bog rubies*. The bright yellows, golds, and reds of the autumn trees accentuated them. During the next few days, Riley, Grandpa, family, and friends would be busy with the laborious task of harvesting the berries. First, they would flood the beds with water from the reservoir using the new pump.

Riley had hired help three weeks ago to assist Grandpa with inspecting the cleaning machine and conveyor and to make sure spare parts were on hand. Once the process began, the crop would not wait while repairs were made. She'd prepared meals to feed the workers ahead of time and frozen them.

It occurred to her that her grandfather had purposefully failed to mention the impending harvest when he'd invited Eric to stay. He probably expected Eric to join in the work like the others. She laughed out loud at the ridiculous thought of her all-business ex-boyfriend knee deep in water, booming the berries. She hoped the labor involved would be enough to send him away.

Weariness filled her at the thought of the endless hours of work that would consume her over the next two or three days. At least less time would be needed since Grandpa's antique walk-behind harvester had been replaced with a new riding one, though they would use the old one as well. She was thrilled that she could be part of her grandfather's life and the farm once again. She never dreamed her world would change so dramatically in such a short period of time.

Moisture brimmed in her eyes. She believed that leaving behind the corporate stress and Eric and moving to this peaceful farm was the answer she was looking for. But as she walked along the dikes, she realized she didn't even know the question. All she knew was that she longed for an inner peace, yet even as a Christian, she felt as though peace eluded her.

As she drew in a deep breath, the earthy smell relaxed her. She could at least try to pray. *Father, please bless my grandfather's cranberry crop and help him build the legacy he's desired for so many years. Please help me to be a good mother to little Chad. And help Zane to know You in a deeper way. Please keep us in the palms of Your hands and protect us.*

Riley swiped her wet eyes then opened them.

A blurred figured in a business suit approached. She sighed with relief when she recognized Zane rather than Eric.

His professional appearance surprised her. She'd grown accustomed to the farm work clothes and admitted she liked him better in them. "What's with the suit? Did you have a meeting this afternoon?"

He cocked his head. The warmth in his eyes had disappeared. "As a matter of fact, I've contacted a security company to install an alarm at both your office and home. But you have to remember to arm it or else it won't work."

Though the vandalism was not something to laugh about, his tone brought a chuckle from her. "You say that as if you know from experience."

His expression looked serious, scolding her lightheartedness. "Last night I returned to my condo to find it in worse shape than your office."

She inhaled sharply. "Oh no! . . . Zane. . .I'm so sorry to hear that."

"I've hired a private investigator."

His news stunned her. "You did? Do you think that will make any difference?"

Zane reached into his suit pocket and pulled out a gold necklace.

Riley scrunched her face. "What's that for?"

"I have a photo that John claimed was you, but it's not. The woman is wearing a gold chain like this, only it also has a locket on it. Do you know where the locket is?"

Riley racked her memory then shook her head. "Sorry, Zane. I've never seen that before. Why are you so sure that I would have it?"

Zane stared off in the distance, frowning. Riley was certain her exasperation mirrored his. "John said he'd sent you something. This is part of the clue. It has to be the locket. You have to have it if we are going to resolve this."

His cold stare sent a chill over her. What had happened to the warm and friendly Zane with the magnetic smile? She couldn't hide her disappointment.

She touched his arm. "If it will make you feel better, I'll look through my stuff. I still have boxes to unpack. Can you believe it? I just—I don't remember getting anything from him. But I could have been distracted with attending his funeral and the move here."

His sympathetic smile encouraged her that the Zane she'd come to know was somewhere inside. She wondered if Eric's appearance had anything to do with Zane's sudden change toward her. Or maybe his friendliness had been part of his ruse to gain access to the farm in his search. Now that she was aware of his scheme, he no longer needed to pretend.

He stared at the ground and kicked at an errant weed with his polished black shoe. He reminded Riley of a little boy who'd been caught stealing candy.

"There's something else."

Here it comes. She shook her head and turned her back to

him, not knowing if she could handle anything else.

"What is it?" Her voice came out breathy, weary.

"Remember when I told you that after your brother left you a message that night he said to himself it could be a matter of life or death? I've believed from the beginning that John's death was no accident."

The meaning of his words gripped her mind and took root. Stunned, she whirled to face him. "Wha–?" The strength in her legs gave out, and she plummeted.

Zane caught her and pulled her to him, maintaining a tight hold as she sobbed against his expensive designer suit.

All the anxiety and worries she'd kept inside in an effort to remain strong rushed out. Questions and accusations reeled in her mind, tormenting her soul. John murdered? Sarah, too? Or had she just been in the wrong place? It was too much to grasp. Her heart ached for her brother's family, for Chad.

Lord, why has this happened?

Zane's voice continued to comfort and soothe in the background of her anguish. When her tears were spent, remorse filled her that she'd exposed her emotions to Zane, and she pushed away from him. She avoided looking at the damage she'd done to his suit.

She pulled a tissue out of her pocket that she kept on hand for Chad and wiped her eyes and nose. "Who, Zane? Who killed my brother? Do the police believe this?"

He gripped her shoulders. "Calm down. One question at a time. I haven't exactly shared my theory with the police."

"What? Why not?"

"Because John left his clues for us to decipher. Not the police. Besides, all I have is suspicions, nothing concrete."

"So what? Isn't that their job to figure out?"

Releasing his hold, he sighed heavily. "But all I have is

something John said and his clues—or at least one of them. Let's go with what John's given us first."

He stepped closer and peered into her eyes. "I didn't want to tell you this because I wanted to spare you, but I feel I've lost enough of your trust already."

❧

Zane's heart ached as he looked at Riley's contorted, pain-filled expression. Anger surged through him that he'd decided to reveal his belief that her brother was murdered. Had his reasons for telling her been all wrong? He'd wanted to regain her trust. Instead, his decision had caused her more pain.

"I should go. I've hurt you enough for one week." He started back to the office, where he'd parked in the drive.

"Wait."

Zane closed his eyes. He didn't know why she'd said the word, but it pleased him. He turned to look at her.

"Could you walk with me a bit? Unless, that is, you have to work." A tight smile tugged at her cheeks.

At the moment, Zane couldn't think of anything he'd rather do than be with her. Nor could he recall any other pressing business for the day. He offered his arm. "Shall we?"

She wiped her eyes again then hooked her arm through his. Though they strolled without speaking, a quiet comfort settled over Zane, and he hoped she felt it, as well. He thought of things to say, conversation starters, but didn't want to disturb the mood. Riley needed time to assimilate what he'd told her.

Their walk took them to the acreage beyond the cranberries amid an abundance of colorful oaks and maples.

When Riley stopped, she faced Zane and grinned. "Sorry about your suit. Do you think you can get that out?"

He glanced down at his soiled shoulder. "This old thing?" The words reminded him of the chocolate incident, and when he saw the sparkle in her eyes, he knew she'd remembered, as well. They both laughed.

"That's a good sound to hear from you. I'm worried about you." He tipped her chin with his thumb to scrutinize her tearstained face. "You know if there was any other way, I wouldn't have told you."

The diminutive smile on her face faded. "You have to tell me everything. I'm a big girl. You shouldn't have kept anything from me. He may have been your partner, but he was my brother." Her lip quivered, but she breathed in and controlled her emotions.

Though Riley's earlier outburst was understandable considering the news he'd given, he admired her attempts to remain strong. But he worried that she allowed herself no outlet.

She closed her eyes as if considering her next words. "If whoever killed my brother is searching for this, aren't we in the same danger?"

"Honestly, I think they realize their mistake in losing John. He was the brilliance they needed to complete their project. I don't think they will make that mistake again."

"Some family and friends helping with the harvest will be arriving tonight."

"You'll be safe surrounded by people."

"What I mean is that I won't have much time to find that locket. That's the key to all of this, isn't it?"

Her concerned expression ripped through the barrier of his control, and he placed his hand gently at the back of her head, pulling her toward him as he wove his fingers through her hair.

She didn't resist.

Her soft lips beckoned him, and he leaned down to meet them, pressing his own against their warmth. Powerful emotions erupted in his soul from the simple touch of his lips against hers.

He released her and backed away, swallowing to fight the sudden dryness in his mouth. "I shouldn't have done that. Forgive me. You're in an awful state of mind. I didn't mean to take advantage of you."

He thrust his hands into his pockets. "We should get back."

Riley appeared dazed at his actions, shoving his guilt deeper. What more could he do to hurt her?

fourteen

Wearing waders the next day, Zane stood knee deep in the bog and wiped the sweat from his forehead with a gloved hand. After several hours of pumping water from the reservoir into each of the beds, he was spent. But daylight remained, and Robert Sanderford had finished his turn driving the eggbeater, a machine that spun reels to churn the water. Zane needed to try his hand at it.

In one of the other beds, Gerome Mays, a distant cousin, used the old walk-behind harvester. Though it took longer, it still accomplished the task. Zane climbed onto the tractor, not much larger than a riding lawn mower, and began the process of stirring up the water. Liberated berries already bunched together, floating in the bog like pieces of a jigsaw puzzle. The machine chugged along at two miles an hour. Zane watched in amazement as the ripe berries, filled with small pockets of air, floated to the top after they separated from the vines.

Once he felt comfortable with the machinery, he allowed his thoughts to drift, mesmerized by the noisy engine and the reel agitating the bog. Despite the burden of knowledge he shared with Riley regarding the events surrounding John's death, they both needed the break that concentrating on the harvest brought. Working with his hands was good therapy.

Riley paced along the dike as if she were on the sidelines watching a football game and waved at him, cheering him on. Her face was bright with excitement, and he was pleased that she'd been able to take her mind off their predicament. Seeing her observe him caused a sense of pride to swell in his chest. Being able to witness the fruits of their labor and take part in the harvest filled his heart with more joy than any business endeavor he'd achieved in the past.

As he turned the machine in the bog, he considered that the true meaning of life had evaded him. What good was it to be a successful businessman if you had no one to share life with? He frowned, his thoughts agitated like the water beneath him. Though he'd paid for Cyphorensic Technologies' office lease a year in advance because he was offered a deal for doing so, without software and a programmer of John's caliber, there was no company. Could he find an adequate replacement for John?

He noticed Riley again. This time she held Chad in her arms, and he waved at Zane. He smiled at his little guy.

His little guy?

Zane's heart warmed at the thought. He admitted he'd grown to love Chad as if he were his own. His gaze wandered back to Riley. Without a thriving business, he believed he couldn't offer them a future. More than anything, he wanted to give her security, stability.

When he glanced back to the dike, Riley and Chad had disappeared. Just as well, because he didn't need the distraction. He'd never intended to work at Sanderford Farms for this long. But he had expected to complete his search before now. Once the harvest was over and he finally presented the business plan to Riley, there was no reason for him to stay on.

He turned the machine again and saw Riley standing on the opposite bank, Eric at her side. Zane allowed a low growl to escape, knowing it wouldn't be heard over the eggbeater's racket. He didn't trust Eric and didn't understand why the man insisted on pursuing Riley when it was clear she had no interest. At least Zane hoped it was clear. Maybe he was only fooling himself. Eric could be the sort of man Riley needed. She had to think of what was best for Chad. Eric had a job. Zane had a defunct company. Still, he didn't like Eric.

Riley smiled at Eric, and they walked off together. Zane cared deeply for Riley, and he wondered why it took Eric's appearance to make him realize how much. He scowled as he watched Eric put his arm around her and pull her close to him as they strolled away. He couldn't believe the man had the audacity to show up at the harvest and not be prepared to get his hands dirty.

The churning complete for this bog, Zane stopped, engaged a lever to lift the reel out of the water, then turned off the engine. He dismounted, stepping into the floating rubies. Gerome's wife, Leiann, stood on the dry dike and offered Zane a large Styrofoam cup.

Eager to drink, he nodded his thanks then gulped the cool, tart lemonade. When he finished, he smiled. "Thanks. I guess I was too thirsty to speak."

She gestured to the house, a twinkle in her hazel eyes. "The women have pulled out the snack trays if you'd like to take a break."

Zane glanced at the bog where Gerome still labored. "What about your husband? Maybe I should go take his place while he eats."

"No, no. I gave him a bite before he started." She looked down at her feet then back at Zane. "I've got on my waders, so I can take him a drink."

Zane headed toward the house, wondering if he would have any time alone with Riley. He hadn't heard if she'd discovered anything, though he was certain she would tell him. But with a home full of cranberry harvest workers, some of whom would remain at the house for the next several days until the task was complete, he doubted she'd had ample opportunity to look.

As he approached the gathering, he saw Riley exit the back door with a covered dish. She set it on a long table covered with food. Friends and family members congregated around the tables; some entered the house itself. Zane washed his hands in the portable washbasin then found the large jug of lemonade and refilled his cup. He maneuvered his way through the friendly faces whose names he was only beginning to learn and approached Riley at the far end of the table. She was uncovering the plastic wrap from a dish of cheese-filled celery.

Zane stood next to her and faced the small gathering that he'd decided yesterday was too large for the required work. But he supposed it was tradition and a reason to bring people together.

One of Robert's church friends picked a piece of celery off the serving dish. Zane smiled at him before finishing off his lemonade. The man ambled down the table, selecting food and placing it on his plate.

Zane caught Riley's attention. "How are you?"

"I'm fine, thanks. But I think we're past the small talk, don't you?"

Her comment startled him. Something was definitely agitating her. He studied her before tilting his cup to toss the remaining ice into his mouth. He crunched on it. "All right, then. Have you found anything?"

"Are you serious? I did as much as I could before this harvest business escalated. It's really bad timing if you ask me. You should have told me everything weeks ago."

Again, Riley's feisty words startled Zane, and he stopped smiling at the people mingling and eating and faced her. She wore a peculiar expression on her face that he couldn't read.

He gripped her elbow and ushered her away from her serving position to the side of the house. "What's going on? Is everything all right? I mean, besides finding the locket. I already know that part of the equation."

"Sorry, I'm tired. And we still have several days to go. I'm not used to this continual labor. . .and entertaining. But don't get me wrong—it's fun in its own way. Besides, this is the life I've chosen, and I'm sure I will grow to love it." She stared at him, and he caught the flicker of a question cross her features. "Next year, that is."

"Yeah, next year." Zane hesitated, considering his words. "You'll be okay, you know? Things are progressing very well on the farm. You have a feel for how to run things now. And you can always call me if you need me." He cringed, wishing he hadn't said it. It sounded too. . .final.

A swaggering peacock dressed in a dark blue polo shirt and tan slacks approached from a distance. *Eric.* Zane scowled.

"What's wrong?" Riley spun to look and released a slight groan.

He suspected her agitation had more to do with her ex-boyfriend than with the requirements of the harvest. He'd been surprised when she explained her previous relationship to Eric. Zane couldn't imagine her falling for someone like him.

"Hi there, Zane." Eric nodded and sidled up to Riley.

Zane stifled the smirk that threatened to erupt when he saw Riley's subtle shudder. "Hi there, yourself."

"How does it feel to work on a cranberry farm?" Eric smiled and cocked his head as if interested in Zane's reply.

"It's hard work, but I've enjoyed it." Remembering his earlier annoyance with Eric's unwillingness to help, he added,

"You might try it yourself."

He instantly regretted the words. Riley stood slightly behind Eric and glared at Zane. The last thing he wanted was to have Eric get involved with the farm. Evidently, Riley felt the same way.

⁂

At home that night, Zane scrubbed the grime off and dressed. He'd received a phone call from Tom Ackley, the private investigator he'd hired. He was pleased that Tom had done such quick work, though he wouldn't give Zane the specifics over the phone. After arming his upgraded security system, Zane headed to a nearby grocery store parking lot.

He sat down in Tom's midsize car and nodded at the man in the driver's seat. "Tom."

"Thanks for meeting me." He wore an expensive suit similar to the design that Zane preferred.

An executive friend working for one of Zane's previous employers had given him Tom's name. "No problem. I hired you, remember?"

Tom chuckled at Zane's comment.

"What have you discovered?" Zane's palms grew moist with the anticipation of possible answers to this dilemma.

Tom pulled a manila folder from the space between his seat and the console. He retrieved the photo of the woman whom John claimed was his sister.

"Did you find out who she is? What's her name and connection to all of this?"

Tom frowned. "You're not going to like it."

Pain erupted in Zane's stomach, and he pressed his hand on his midsection then leaned against the headrest.

The private investigator handed him another picture. It was smooth and glossy, cut from a magazine. "The February edition of *Tech-It* magazine."

"What? Are you saying that the photo on John's desk is not a real person?"

"It is a real person. . .a model. I'm saying this photo is an image taken from that magazine. Maybe your partner thought she looked like his sister, and since he didn't have a picture, he used this."

Zane couldn't hide the disappointment in his voice. "Thanks for the work, Tom. Do you have anything else?"

"Not yet."

"All right, then."

The two men nodded, and Zane exited Tom's vehicle to climb into his own and head home. He'd needed to check whether the woman's identity was also part of the clue. John had created a photo-quality image from a picture in a magazine for use in his insane puzzle. Why? Though Zane still ached for his friend, he hoped that wherever John was right now, he could look on and get some sort of satisfaction out of knowing that Zane and Riley were striving to solve the puzzle. Zane remembered the regret Riley expressed because she hadn't discussed God with John. The thought left him unsettled.

He was beginning to see that he couldn't manage his life on his own. But he'd kept himself closed off from God for so long that he didn't know where to begin.

༚

Riley gripped the floating rubber tube called a boom as she helped the others corral the crimson sheet of bog rubies close to the conveyor belt that would propel them onto a platform. Booming the berries had always fascinated her as a child, but she'd never been allowed to help with this part of the harvest. Urging the berries forward in the water took more strength than she would have thought. Though Grandpa had protested at her involvement because there were plenty of other workers to help, she held her ground, wanting to experience everything.

She caught sight of Chad standing next to Millie and Elsie, and she waved at him. She hoped he would grow up enjoying the experience of the cranberry farm as she had. Once the berries were tightly packed, floating near the equipment, Zane, Grandpa, and others moved inside the circle to begin scraping the carpet of crimson fruit onto the belt, where they were cleaned. When the platform had reached its capacity, the contents were dumped into the freight car of an 18-wheeler that was then sent to one of the independent cranberry handlers.

Grandpa did not belong to the large co-op with which 70 percent of the Massachusetts cranberry growers were contracted. The cost to join was high, and he wouldn't get paid until the cranberries were actually sold by the handler. She intended to speak with Zane for his business advice on whether to remain independent or belong to the co-op. The advantage of joining would be a three-year, fixed-rate contract.

Riley labored alongside the others for two more days. Though she enjoyed every minute of it, the entire process was all-consuming. They'd already said good-bye to several of their helpers as the bogs began to empty and the guests began to vacate the house.

Too exhausted to remove her waders, she meandered away from the activity toward the grove of trees where Zane had kissed her. She could still feel the warmth that had flooded her being at his tenderness, even though it had been a few days ago. If only the kiss had occurred under different circumstances than after learning that he believed her brother was murdered. But his response to his actions had left her confused about his feelings and intentions.

The gloomy thought that she hadn't asked about her brother's relationship with the Lord continued to surface, bothering her. Yet it also reminded her that she needed to broach the subject with Zane, as well. Time after time, she'd worked up the courage to speak with Zane, but he'd continued to change the subject or allow other interruptions. She had to know before she allowed her feelings to go any deeper for him. Already the man had made inroads into her heart without her realizing how far.

All she had longed for was a simple life. Instead, her life had become more complicated since the day Zane arrived at Sanderford Cranberry Farms.

fifteen

"Nonsense, we can go together." Grandpa paced in the kitchen, dressed in his best jeans for the harvest festival.

"You're all ready to go, though. It's going to take me awhile. Call your church friends back, Grandpa."

For the last few years, the largest cranberry grower in the region hosted a festival for all to celebrate the harvest. She wanted to be excited, but she was too exhausted. If it weren't for the fact that she'd agreed to meet Zane there, she would skip it altogether.

Riley handed Chad his juice cup then rubbed her aching head. The harvest had zapped all her energy. Though the crop had been trucked off the farm two days before, she still hadn't recovered.

Grandpa came to Riley and placed his hand on her shoulder. "All right, then. I'll go without you. But only because I can see you need a little time to yourself." He grinned and gave her a loving pat.

"You'd better hurry before they leave without you," she said.

"How about I take little Chad with us. Millie will be there. She loves to see him."

"What about her granddaughter, Elsie?" Relief washed over Riley. She longed to soak in a hot bath to ease her aching muscles. She couldn't help but smile about the fact that her grandfather had grown to like Millie, after all. He'd made healthy progress, finally getting on with his life after the death of her grandmother. She grinned when she considered that much of that growth had occurred since she'd arrived.

"I'm sure she'll be there, too. Don't worry about us; we'll have a good time."

"Let me grab his things, and don't forget to take the car seat," she said.

After seeing Chad and Grandpa off, Riley locked the door and bounded upstairs to start her bathwater. She'd spent yesterday rummaging through her things, including the ten moving boxes that had remained in the garage, still packed. Though her heart ached for her brother—and even more now that Zane had told her he believed John was murdered—she began to feel angry with John about the mystery he expected her and Zane to solve. She couldn't understand why he hadn't spelled things out so they could understand.

Riley soaked in the tub until the water turned cold. The bath eased her tension, and she felt relaxed. She even sent up a silent prayer for the discovery of the elusive clue. In the mood to look special, she searched through the closet, looking at her nicer clothes that she hadn't worn in months, since caring for a child left a spot on every shirt she owned.

She held a tan outfit against her body and stared at the mirror, frowning. The pantsuit needed something extra, maybe jewelry. She hoped to look special for Zane.

For Zane?

Shaking her head, she tugged a dresser drawer open to dig out the jewelry box buried underneath a jumble of undergarments. She tossed them into a cardboard box nestled beside the dresser so that she could get a better look at the contents of the disorganized drawer.

She froze. The cardboard box had rested in that spot for

so long that it had become part of the room's decor and had gone unnoticed. She hadn't searched it. Still, it only contained items she'd tossed in recently. She grabbed it and dumped the contents onto the bed. Along with the clothes, several postmarked envelopes—junk mail and solicitations—were scattered amid the heap, and she gathered them together, tossing them as she searched for a letter from John.

One envelope did not have a return address but had been sent to Riley's California address. It had been forwarded to Massachusetts. Then she noticed the Massachusetts postmark. In the midst of all the turmoil, she'd overlooked the letter. The handwriting appeared to be that of a man. Her heart pounded as she searched for a letter opener to slit the top. She hoped this was the item John had sent.

Losing patience, Riley ripped through the paper. She pulled out several folded sheets and discovered a small item in between them.

The locket!

As she examined the shiny, gold-plated square, touching it with her finger, she couldn't believe she had finally found it. Still, what could be so important about a trivial ornament?

She scrutinized the sliding door in the front of the locket. Riley's heart raced. Should she open it or wait for Zane? Upon applying slight pressure with her thumb, the door slid open, and a small square object dropped to the carpet. Riley reached down and carefully picked up what appeared to be the smallest memory card she'd ever seen. It was no bigger than her fingernail.

Fear coursed through her. The information she held in the palm of her hand had meant the difference between life and death to John. Her mood plummeted. Somehow, things had gone awry. She hated that she was in possession of such a dangerous object.

She hurried to dress so she could deliver the news to Zane. The locket would be the perfect accessory to her tan outfit— sure to draw his attention. The ironic notion brought a laugh. Zane had kept the original golden chain he'd shown her. Riley came across one of an appropriate length, though it was silver rather than gold like the locket.

She phoned Zane on his cell. When he didn't answer, she left a message on his voice mail. She tried to keep her voice calm, rather than shaky, but it was no use.

੨ৱ

Zane tired of the culinary demonstration and roamed toward the farm stand, avoiding the live band that played on the temporary stage. He scanned the crowd for Riley. He assumed she would have arrived at the festival by now. He checked his watch and noted that dusk was fast approaching. A helicopter offering rides zoomed past, rendering him momentarily oblivious to any other sounds.

A young girl approached him holding glowing neon bracelets and sticks. "Mister, would you like to buy one?"

He patted the young entrepreneur on the top of her head. "No, thanks. Maybe later."

As he sauntered down a walkway rimmed by people pushing their wares, he looked at all sorts of antiques, linens, artwork, and even produce from the local farmers. Completing the harvest had filled him with satisfaction. The celebration festival was for all to enjoy. Without Riley, there wasn't much here to interest Zane. He checked his watch again then spotted her grandfather.

He hurried through the crowd before he lost sight of

Robert then touched the back of his arm. Riley's grandfather turned to face Zane, his broad smile growing even bigger.

"Hello, Robert. Enjoying the festival?"

"Grandpa! Grandpa!" Chad came running from a vendor, a stick of pink-and-blue-swirled cotton candy in his hand. Millie wasn't far behind the child. Riley would be near, as well.

A pang jolted Zane's heart at Chad's outburst—he'd begun calling Robert "Grandpa," which was only right. But the child would grow up and not even remember his own father. Still, Zane was grateful that the boy had family to love him.

Robert lifted Chad into his arms, heedless of the sticky mess. Yes, he was loved.

"There's a huge crowd this year. Have you been to a cranberry festival before?" Robert opened his mouth to allow Chad to stuff in the sticky sugar.

"I'm afraid this is my first time." Zane watched Millie retrieve Chad from Robert's arms. Something was going on between those two. He grinned at the thought.

"So, do you know which way Riley headed? I'm surprised I haven't seen her yet."

A nearby carnival ride began booming upbeat music.

"What?" Robert appeared to consider Zane's question. "I'm not sure where Riley is. I haven't seen her. She decided to come later."

Robert's words sank in, filling Zane with disappointment. He frowned and searched the crowd. "How would we find her in all of this, even if she was here?"

"That's a good question. But I wouldn't worry too much. I think she needed time alone. She worked hard. I can't tell you how proud I was to see her standing in the bogs, booming the berries. It was a grand time for all of us." Robert slapped Zane on the back.

Though he knew Riley's grandfather meant to encourage him, Zane became concerned. "I think I'll walk around and look for her."

"All right, son. We'll tell her that you're looking for her if she turns up."

Zane moved closer to the entrance so he could see Riley in case she entered the festivities. In the distance, he spotted Eric strolling the grounds, searching the crowd, no doubt looking for Riley, the same as Zane. He melted back into the shadows. What was Eric doing here? Riley had said he'd returned to California.

Zane didn't feel he could stomach Eric at the moment. He wondered if his enormous dislike for the man could be attributed to the intense jealousy he felt when he saw the two of them together. He wondered if the insane emotion had clouded his judgment of Eric and whether in any other circumstances they might be friends.

He doubted it.

Zane decided to call Riley. When he pulled his cell out of his pocket, he saw that he'd missed a call from her. He surmised that bursts of loud music, helicopter rides, or the throng had distracted him when she'd called. His concern mounting, he hoped it wasn't important and that she only meant to tell him she was on the way or already there.

He dialed into voice mail then saw Riley moving between people. She appeared flushed and anxious. He stepped from the building's edge where he'd hidden from Eric, only to witness the man edge toward Riley. When Eric reached his prey ahead of Zane, Riley visibly stiffened. At least Zane had no reason to be jealous.

He realized what nagged him about Eric. Riley's distaste for him had become apparent to all. Zane could not believe a man with Eric's intelligence would not heed the signals Riley sent him. Yet here he was, three thousand miles from his home, pursuing a disinterested female.

As Zane watched Eric head to the Ferris wheel with Riley in tow, he wondered what the man was after.

sixteen

Eric tightened his grip on Riley's elbow as he ushered her toward the Ferris wheel. She glared at him. "You're hurting me. What's the matter with you?"

His expression turned ominous, sending panic through her. "We need to talk."

Her ex-boyfriend's grip remained unyielding as they stood in line. To Riley's dismay, Eric had timed his carnival ride excursion at the right moment, and after a quick word with the ride operator, they were quickly escorted into a cozy car all to themselves.

She buckled in and leaned back against the red vinyl cushion, wondering what had just happened. Her intentions had been to find Zane and tell him she had discovered the locket that held the key to their mystery. Within the few minutes of her arrival at the festival, the horde of people had grown, and she'd shuffled along with them in her search for Zane. Oh, how she wished she'd found Zane before Eric had appeared out of nowhere.

He was scaring her.

She twisted a small topaz ring on her finger, avoiding Eric's stare, then mustered her courage and raised her head to face him. "I thought you'd gone back to California, that the work that brought you to Boston was finished. Surely you can't still be taking time off. What are you doing here?"

"No, Riley, I'm not vacationing. As a matter of fact, I didn't accomplish the work I flew here to do. Yet."

Riley shifted in her seat under his menacing gaze. The carnival worker finished loading excited passengers on the wheel, and it began to rotate. A breeze lifted Riley's hair from her face, cooling her.

A pleasant tune signaled a caller on her cell. Her heart skipped, hoping it was Zane. His number appeared in the small window. She pressed the RECEIVE button. "This is Riley."

"Are you all right?" Zane's voice barreled through the phone, wrapping her in assurance.

She looked at Eric, who watched her like a bird of prey, readying to strike. She measured her words carefully. "I'm. . . fine, thanks. Where are you?"

"I'm down below. If you look out, you can see me." Riley leaned to the side but saw no one she recognized in the crowd. "I'm sorry, there are too many people. But it's good to know you're there." She looked at Eric again. For some reason, she feared he might grab the phone from her. She tightened her grip then banished the ridiculous thought.

"I saw you come in, but then Eric rushed you onto the Ferris wheel before I could get to you."

His words warmed her. If only he had made it in time. "The ride will be over soon enough."

"Hang in there." He laughed. "Sorry, I didn't mean to make a joke out of it. I called because you looked. . .uncomfortable."

"That's putting it mildly, but you're right, this, too, shall pass. I'll see you on the ground. Oh, wait!" Riley could not tell Zane of her discovery with Eric listening. "I left you a voice mail. Did you get it?"

A barrage of noise invaded her phone, and she couldn't hear Zane's voice. She'd lost the connection, so she pressed the END button.

Feeling confident after Zane's encouragement, she glared at

Eric. "You still haven't answered my question. What are you doing here? I know you have no interest in this festival. And you should know by now that I have no interest in you."

A condescending grin spread over his mouth. "I assure you, the feeling is quite mutual."

Stunned by his comment and his strange behavior, she didn't know how to respond and instead watched the beautiful scenery as the wheel made its way around. While she gathered her thoughts, she stared at the lights glistening in the distance with the falling darkness. The raucous sound of the carnival seemed to grow louder, even at the top of the ride. The aroma of hamburgers and hot dogs drifted up on the breeze.

"I'm sorry, you'll have to explain to me again, then, why you insisted that I ride the wheel with you if you don't enjoy my company," she said.

She'd never seen this side of Eric before, even after all the time she'd spent with him. As memories raced through her mind, she remembered occasions here and there when he'd revealed a different part of himself.

He stared into the distance as if contemplating his response to her. His dark hair rustled in the wind. She examined his handsome profile and considered the fact that the behavior he exhibited tonight had been within him the entire time she'd known him. But her feelings had erased any negative thoughts she may have had at the time because she'd cared about him.

Sitting before her was the real Eric. And she still cared about him as a person who needed God, but no longer as a man she'd once considered spending the rest of her life with, though he'd never asked.

As if in response to her thoughts of marriage, an image of Zane made her heart skip. She shook the presumptuous thought from her mind.

"Where is it?" Eric continued to stare out the side of the car and did not turn when he addressed her.

Immediately her thoughts went to the locket, and she placed her hand over it where it hung around her neck. Panic exploded from within and rushed through her body, sending moisture to her palms and trembling to her limbs. She fought to hide the emotion in her expression and thanked the Lord that Eric had chosen not to look at her.

How does he know?

"What?" she managed to say through an emotion-filled throat.

He picked that moment to face her, but his expression appeared relaxed. "Where is it? You know what I'm talking about." The mocking she'd heard in his earlier tone was gone, but his gaze pierced her, showing that he meant business.

She could not believe her ears. He had nothing to do with any of this. "Eric, I really don't have a clue what you're talking about. Did I take something of yours when I left California? Just tell me. You can have it back!"

"Your brother, John, sent it to you. I want it."

Her mouth went dry as she stared at him. If only he'd asked her yesterday, she could have told him the truth when she said she didn't know where it was. Now if she said that, he would know she was lying. Eric knew her too well.

"I—I don't know what you're talking about." It couldn't hurt to try the tactic once more.

He leaned forward. "Come now, Riley. I know you're lying."

Grief rushed through her soul as realization flooded her mind. She'd been only too thrilled to tell Eric about John's talents and his encryption project. Nausea roiled in her stomach, and she gripped her middle, bending over. Riley had been foolish to think she could share information, even if it was with her boyfriend—someone she thought she could trust.

As a business consultant, Eric had high-level connections, and his knowledge had leaked to the wrong party. She groaned as she continued to clutch her stomach, sick that she had brought this upon her brother. She no longer cared if she exposed her emotions.

The man already knew everything.

Eric unbuckled and moved next to her. He leaned closer and spoke softly into her ear. "If you give it to me, no one else will get hurt."

Images of Chad, Grandpa, and Zane tore through her mind. She cried out to God. What should she do? Would giving the memory card to Eric release them from danger? Or would it put them at further risk? They could tell the police about Eric and his connection with John's murder.

John's smiling face appeared in her mind. How she missed her brother. Fury surged through her that Eric had taken him from her.

She turned to face him, the heat of her rage exploding. "You! You murdered my brother!" She slapped him full across the face.

He covered his cheek with his hand as he winced. "It wasn't me, Riley. I didn't do it. All I did was share information about your brother's skills with an interested client. Believe me, had I known who I was dealing with, well, I would have stayed far away. I'm sorry about that. But it's too late now. They're breathing down my neck to retrieve the information your brother sent you."

His hand dropped to his side, revealing his reddened face. Eric appeared to revert to the man she'd been attracted to months ago. He huffed and rubbed his hands together. "Please understand." He paused as he swept her hair away from her face. "I'm just trying to keep anyone else from getting hurt. Namely, you." He lifted her hand and kissed it.

She knew he intended to turn his charm on her since his fear tactics had not worked, but his touch repulsed her.

She had to get off this ride.

&

Zane's patience ran thin. With the crowd growing for the evening festivities, he couldn't pace as a way of relieving his tension. He'd never realized how many turns a Ferris wheel could take. Maybe it was standard at all carnivals and he hadn't paid attention. He made his way through the line of grumbling people while excusing himself. He explained to any who challenged him that he needed to speak to the carnival employee.

The man stood jesting with another worker and appeared to ignore the Ferris wheel.

"Excuse me, sir," Zane interrupted.

The man shoved his baseball cap up on his head to reveal questioning dark brown eyes. He tilted his head in reply to Zane.

Zane noticed the man's name on his flannel shirt. "Carl, I'm wondering about how long your ride has been running. Please don't misunderstand. I'm not challenging your abilities as a ride operator; I'm just curious. Is this normal?"

Carl's friend slapped his back and left him. Carl returned his attention to Zane and rubbed his gray-stubbled chin. "A guy wanted extra time with his girlfriend." He revealed an impish grin and lifted the corner of a green bill out of his shirt pocket, enough for Zane to see he'd been paid one hundred dollars. "He made it worth my while."

Zane gritted his teeth. "I'll pay you double to stop it."

Carl grinned and rubbed his chin again, as if considering the proposal. Zane surmised that the man didn't intend to make things easy. "All right. I never said how long I would keep it running." He cleared his throat and motioned for Zane to follow him away from the crowd. "You can slip it in my hand. The two hundred dollars, that is."

Zane pulled his wallet from his slacks and unfolded it. Comprehension dawned like the beginning of a bad day. He'd planned to get money at an ATM at the festival, but he'd been consumed with finding Riley.

"I have to get cash."

The man shrugged and started to march back to the waiting line.

As the wheel turned, Zane heard Riley's voice when her car whirled past. She was in distress.

Zane grabbed Carl's arm. "No, wait!"

Carl turned a threatening glare on him, causing Zane to release him. "I'll give you four hundred if you'll stop it while I go get the cash."

"I'm not stopping it until you give me the money."

Incensed, Zane raised his voice. "Look, you're going to have to stop the wheel sooner or later. Look at all those people in line."

Carl shrugged. "It's a carnival; they're used to waiting."

Zane growled at the insensitive ride operator, feeling as though he'd caused the man to run the thing longer than he had planned. He should have waited. He walked away from Carl and rushed over to the operating equipment. In his desperation, he sent up a prayer that he would know how to stop the Ferris wheel before Carl stopped him.

seventeen

The ride wrenched to a stop, sending the cars swinging violently, the huge wheel grinding in protest on its axis. Riley plunged forward, but her safety belt held her, securing her to the seat. The force thrust Eric across the small platform because he'd failed to strap himself back in.

He gripped his head and groaned.

She heard a ruckus below and peered over the edge of the car as far as she could to see what was happening. Two men struggled near the Ferris wheel's operating stand. A familiar tall figure reached for the controls, while the carnival worker wrapped his arms around him, trying to stop him.

"Zane." She drew in a sharp breath.

Other men rushed to them and pulled the two apart. She heard Zane's prominent, authoritative voice taking control of the situation. He pointed at the ride operator and spoke in an accusing tone.

Eric righted himself on the seat. Blood trickled from a gash in his temple. "Your new boyfriend can't save you, Riley. In fact, you're the one who needs to save him. Give me what I want."

Riley looked at Eric, surprised at what she heard in his voice. "You're afraid, aren't you?"

The wheel started again then paused to allow passengers off each of the cars. The process of disembarking the riders continued.

"Yes. I'm afraid. And you should be scared, too." He spat

the words. "Are you happy now?"

Riley closed her eyes, overwhelmed as a sense of peace wrapped around her. She knew that someone had to be praying for her at that moment. She opened her eyes to stare at Eric and realized that she felt sorry for the man.

"Well, I'm not scared. God is going to protect me."

Eric leaned back against the seat and laughed. "When we get off this thing, you're going with me, and I'm going to make you hand over what John gave you."

"Zane will be waiting for me." As soon as the words left her mouth, it was their turn to exit the car.

A man apologized to them for the inconvenience. Riley looked for Zane, expecting him to be waiting for her, but she didn't see him. "Where's the man who was here?"

"Which one, lady?"

"The one—"

Eric thanked the worker and hastened Riley away, his grip tight. Screams of fear and excitement bombarded them as noisy rides thrust their occupants about. Deafening music boomed from all sides. Riley could see how it would be easy for Eric to abduct her in the midst of the throng. No one would even hear her scream.

"Okay, Eric. I give."

He turned to face her and paused to look around at the multitude of festival attendees. "That's better."

"Promise me that no one else will get hurt if I give it to you." She held her breath as she fingered the locket.

"I promise. Do we need to go somewhere, or do you have it with you?"

Riley glared at him, gripping the clue that John had given her and yanking it from her neck.

A disbelieving grin spread across Eric's face, and he released his grip on her. "Oh man, you've got to be kidding me. You were wearing it this whole time?" He glanced behind her and stiffened.

Riley pressed the locket into his hand then darted away from him, rushing through the onslaught of bodies. She dared not look behind her. She ran full force into a man's chest. He gripped her arms and pushed her away to reveal his face.

"Riley?" Zane wrapped his arms around her and held her close.

All the tension of the last hour came flooding out in a torrent. There was nothing she hated more than tears. But she couldn't help the emotional release.

People jostled against them as they stood in the center of the fray.

Riley leaned her head back to see Zane's face. He released her. She looked at his tailored blue shirt.

"You're going to have to toss another one, I'm afraid," she said, sniffling again. She dug through her small purse for a tissue without success.

Zane ushered her over to a bench, grabbing a napkin from a concession stand on the way. "Here, try this."

She took it and wiped her eyes then her nose. "Where were you? I got off the Ferris wheel, and you were gone."

"I'm sorry about that. They took me to the security office where I explained about my response to the ride operator's misconduct. Someone paid him to leave the ride going longer than usual. That kept me from being there to wait for you. I should have left matters well enough alone. The ride would have stopped on its own—eventually."

She blew her nose again. "No, it's okay. You tried."

"Riley, tell me what happened up there. What did Eric want?"

She breathed deeply through her nose. It still made a sniffling sound. "Oh, Zane. You're not going to believe this."

Concern and warmth brimmed in his eyes. "It's all right now. You're okay. I'm not ever going to let that man near you again."

Zane's chivalrous words touched her, and she patted his hand. "Calm down."

He returned her smile but with a question in his eyes.

"I think we've seen the last of Eric," she said.

A child climbed up onto the bench next to Riley and tried to hand her half of his hot dog slathered with mustard and ketchup. His mother squeezed next to him, crowding Riley and Zane.

Zane stood and urged Riley to follow. "Let's find a place where we can talk."

He held her hand as if he was never going to let her go. Yet his touch felt nothing like Eric's unwanted, painful grip.

"What about Chad? Grandpa? I forgot all about them. Have you seen them?"

"Yes, more than an hour ago. They were enjoying themselves. Millie and Robert were taking good care of Chad. I don't think you need to worry about him. He's in good hands."

Riley followed Zane on shaky legs. Her entire body felt like Jell-O, trembling from her encounter with Eric. They found a small coffee kiosk. Riley stayed with Zane while he purchased drinks.

He flashed his card at her. "At least someone here takes these."

They settled nearby at an out-of-the-way picnic table.

"Okay, take a long swig of that. Give it time to clear your mind. Are you hungry? I'm sorry I didn't think of food."

"I couldn't eat right now. My stomach's too upset."

Zane sipped coffee and stared at her over the rim of his cup. She could see that he wasn't going to push her to tell him about Eric. She'd been bursting to tell him her news, and with all that had happened, she wasn't sure where to begin.

In the beginning. . .

The gentle voice nudged her heart, delighting her, and she laughed.

Zane cocked a brow. "Something funny?"

"Nothing, really. I was just wondering where to begin."

"In the beginning."

She nodded. "That's what I hear."

Riley told Zane about Eric's involvement and the part she'd played in her brother's demise.

He reached across the table to hold her hand. "You couldn't have known. Don't blame yourself. John's occupation wasn't a secret."

She relished his comforting words and touch. There was no doubt that she would have to ask God to help her forgive herself. The urge to talk about her relationship with God spilled over, but she bit her lip. She knew Zane wouldn't want to hear it now. But when?

Lord, please help me to speak to him when the time is right.

Nor would he want to hear the worst part of her story. She hesitated while she considered how to break the news to him.

❧

Zane's insides ached as he watched Riley. He was grateful that the scoundrel hadn't hurt her. He played with her fingers, hoping to help her relax. At the same time, he fought his own frustration. It would go a long way to relieve his anger if he could get his own hands on the man responsible for John's death. Yet according to what Riley said, Eric hadn't known anyone would be hurt.

Riley's words that they would not see Eric again echoed through Zane's mind.

Too bad.

Zane froze as the thought grabbed him.

"Riley, why won't we see Eric again?"

"Excuse me?" She drove her fingers through her tousled hair, weaving it out of her face.

"You said we wouldn't see Eric again."

She frowned and took a sip of her coffee.

"Riley. What did you give him?" Zane stood up from the picnic table. "Did you find the locket?"

"Yes, I rushed to the carnival to tell you—then Eric grabbed me." She frowned. "I'm so sorry, Zane. I had no choice."

Zane sunk back to the bench. He was grateful for Riley's safety. That was more important than anything, especially a ridiculous clue. But without the locket, they could go no further in solving John's puzzle.

Riley's eyes widened, and she covered her mouth while she reached into her pocket. "You're right, the coffee helped clear my thoughts. I was so focused on the locket, and Eric upset me. I forgot."

A mischievous smile spread across Riley's face. "I said that I gave him the locket. But I didn't give him this."

She held out her palm. A tiny square rested in the center of her hand.

A memory card.

eighteen

Riley held Zane's hand as she followed him through the festival crowd then to the parking lot. He headed in the opposite direction of her parked car.

"My car is that way," she said.

He continued in the same direction and increased his pace; he noticed Riley lagging behind and pulled her along.

"But what about my car? I could just follow you."

"No way. I'm not letting you out of my sight." Zane opened the door to his car for Riley. "I want you to see this through with me. We can get your car later."

He stroked her cheek with his thumb and pressed his lips into a tight smile.

Riley nodded her agreement and climbed in. She called her grandfather to check on Chad, and she explained about Eric. Millie and several others had stopped over to visit after leaving the festival, relieving her of concerns. She reminded her grandfather to arm the security alarm.

Sooner or later, Eric would discover that she hadn't given him all that he'd asked for. She silently prayed for him, concerned for his life in all this chaos, as well.

She reached under the seat to adjust the legroom and found Zane's computer. He slid into the driver's seat and shut the door.

"Are we going to look at the memory card now?" she asked.

"Afraid I'll have to get an adapter—a card reader. So we're going to an electronics store."

Zane started the car, and they exited the parking lot to head toward Plymouth on Interstate 44.

"So what's stored on this thing? What is so important that it cost John his life?"

"I thought I knew. But I'm not so sure anymore. I've been hoping that John stored an extra copy of the new encryption software so that I would still be able to go forward with the business." He paused as he merged to head north. "But now I don't think I want software that someone is willing to kill for."

"What else could it be?" Riley gripped her seat as Zane passed the slower traffic.

"We'll find out as soon as we see what's on that card. Could be the software itself or other files that John wanted us to see. But there's something else. I haven't told you everything. John had a run-in with the law a few years ago. He illegally hacked into—well, you don't need to know the details."

Riley's curiosity was piqued. "So what are you saying, Zane? That my brother was a hacker and this whole thing has to do with something illegal?"

Zane looked out the driver's window. She wished he'd keep his eyes on the road.

He returned his attention to driving. "It's possible—in fact, it's probable—that Eric's friend wanted John to hack into someone's system. But his moonlighting activities have taken Cyphorensic down with it. It's either that, or they simply wanted what John had been developing for Cyphorensic— a new hack-proof algorithm. Then they could offer it to the highest bidder. But obviously, they're still searching for something. I thought they were looking for the key, because they have his software—they stole the computers, remember?" He chuckled. "But they couldn't get into John's stuff."

"What do you think they're after if not the key?"

"Well, let me just say that we may have the same problem. If the key isn't on the minidisk, then we can't open it."

Riley sighed and stared out the window. She shook her head and frowned, saddened by thoughts of everything that had gone wrong in the last several months.

Still, she had Chad, and her grandfather appeared to be happy. The same peace that surrounded her while she was in Eric's company on the Ferris wheel burned inside her. She turned to look at Zane, who concentrated on driving.

"Something happened to me while I was with Eric." She looked out the window again.

"I'm sorry I didn't stop him from taking you on that ride. You're okay, aren't you? He didn't physically hurt you, did he?" Zane placed his right hand over hers and steered with his left one.

"No, nothing like that. In fact, it has nothing to do with Eric."

"I'm listening." He shot her a wry grin.

Riley hesitated, considering how to explain it. "I hated my life in California. I was so preoccupied with my job that I barely had time for myself. And no time for my relationship with God." She held her breath, waiting to sense any tension in Zane as she broached the subject.

When he said nothing, she continued. "I wanted to break up with Eric. In fact, I did, but he wouldn't accept it. I thought coming all the way across the country and giving up my career would change things. I believed living with Grandpa and working the farm would bring back the wonderful feelings I had when I was a child."

"Riley, we're all looking for anything to fill the void, to make us happy." Zane exited the freeway, drove down the frontage road, and turned right, into a large shopping center.

"When I finally moved here, I prayed and read my Bible. It was almost as though I was trying to force things to happen."

He frowned as he pulled into a parking spot.

"Zane, I found it. I found the peace I've been looking for."

He smiled. "You're coming in, right? I wouldn't want to leave you out here by yourself."

He started to open the door, but Riley grabbed his arm. "Please let me finish."

"All right." Zane shifted in his seat, turning his full attention to Riley.

Riley's heart warmed to think that he was willing to listen, though he had to be anxious to review the information on the disk. But she felt a heavenly urge to tell him everything.

"I found that peace when I was on the Ferris wheel with Eric. I finally understood God's peace could come in the midst of striving. It's not a matter of what's going on around me—if I'm busy or if I'm not. It's a matter of what's going on inside of me and if I'm able to receive His peace in all circumstances."

He narrowed his eyes as if contemplating her words. "And what about now? Do you feel it?"

She nodded and grinned. "I do."

He gripped the steering wheel and stared out the windshield. "Well, at least one of us has found the answer. Shall we go?"

She swallowed the sudden knot in her throat and got out of the vehicle. His response was not what she'd expected. Still, she knew she'd done the right thing by telling him of her experience. God would have to do the rest.

They rushed into the large discount electronics and appliance store. Zane headed straight for the ministorage devices and searched the aisle.

A store clerk wearing a red polo shirt joined them. "Can I help you find something?"

Zane glanced at the man's name tag and held the memory card up between his fingers. "Yes, Darryl, I need an adapter to run this on my laptop."

❧

Zane got into the car and tossed the small sack containing the adapter in the backseat. He'd hated the disillusioned expression on Riley's face when he hadn't responded as she expected. He was happy that Riley had found contentment. And. . .it gave him hope.

He started the car. "You ready?"

She nodded, appearing preoccupied.

"Do you think your grandfather would mind if we did this at the farm?"

Her eyes widened; then she smiled. "You know he wouldn't. Thanks. I mean, for thinking of me. I'd like to check on Chad."

"Thought so. We need to be there, too, in case Eric shows up again." Zane put pressure on the accelerator to bring them to the speed limit. In less than half an hour, he could have the information in his hands that could solve John's puzzle.

They rode in comfortable silence, though Riley's words about finding God's peace would not be quieted in his mind. He glanced over at her several times as she stared out the passenger window.

"All right." He winced, wondering if he was making a mistake. But Riley had come to mean more to him than anything. He didn't want to let her down. He could at least try—for her.

"All right, what?"

"All right. If it's time to talk about God, I'm ready."

A beautiful, breathtaking smile filled her face, and the previous stress appeared to melt away, revealing an inner glow. No, this idea had not been a mistake.

"I grew up in church. My mother made sure to take me every Sunday, so I thought I knew God, or at least that I knew who He was." His throat tightened as the memories he'd pushed down for years began to surface.

"It's really strange, but the last person I spoke to about this was your brother, years ago when we were in high school."

A look of awe crossed her face. She moved her lips as if in silent prayer. "I'm glad you're telling me this."

Zane took the exit to head back to Carver and Sanderford Cranberry Farms. "My brother drowned when he was a senior. I looked up to him, idolized him. He was only two years older than me and on the swim team. Can you believe it?"

Though the words came out with difficulty, Zane found that an enormous weight began to lift as he shared with Riley. "We all took it hard, of course, but none took it harder than my father. He had big plans for my brother, and when he looked at me, his entire attitude changed. I thought he wished I had died instead."

Riley placed her hand on his arm. "Oh, Zane, you must be mistaken. I'm sure he loved you very much."

"I know you mean well, but you didn't know my father. He ended up leaving us—me and my mother. Don't misunderstand; my father was wealthy, and we were well taken care of, but he divorced my mother and moved to Europe. I never saw him again. All I have left of him is the money he willed to me when he died four years ago."

"And your mother? Where is she now?"

"A cemetery near Plymouth."

Silence filled the vehicle, but this time, tension accompanied it. Zane knew the tension emanated from him alone.

"If you're wondering what this has to do with God, I'll tell you. I couldn't understand why my brother died and my father left. Why should I count on God after He let me down? So rather than relying on Him, I've relied on myself, working hard to make it where I am today." The words sounded crass even to his own ears.

Riley gasped. "But, Zane, you can count on Him."

"That's what your brother told me." He turned into the entrance of the farm and continued toward the house.

"What did you say?"

Zane glanced at Riley, and the look of wonderment on her face took him by surprise.

"Your brother told me that I can count on God and His Son. John was there for me during that difficult time in my life and has been my closest friend since. That is, until he died."

"Zane, I know what you must think. That whether John was killed in an accident or murdered, how can you count on God? But we don't see the larger picture around us. He was there for me on the Ferris wheel with Eric. I know it."

&.

John was a Christian!

Zane's words thrilled Riley, and she wanted to weep for joy, but she'd cried enough for one day.

As Zane pulled around the circular drive to park near the house, Millie and her granddaughter stepped through the door. Riley got out of the car.

Millie came over to hug her, a large handbag hooked in her elbow. "Riley, dear, I just put Chad down. Your grandfather was a bit nervous. Afraid he wouldn't be able to get the poor child to sleep, so Elsie and I stayed to keep him company."

"Oh, thank you. I'm sorry I'm so late. Did Chad do all right, then?"

Millie waved her hand to throw off any doubt. "He was a complete angel. Exhausted, but an angel. We were just leaving, but come inside, and I'll show you what I've done. I prayed for you this evening, dear. Don't know why but just felt I needed to do it. Is everything all right?"

Warmth filled Riley at Millie's words. "Everything is fine. Thank you for your prayers. I felt them."

Riley noticed Zane removing his briefcase and his purchase from the car as she followed Millie into the house.

Once in the kitchen, the older woman pointed out a large plate of chocolate chip cookies. "I made grilled cheese sandwiches, too, thinking you might be hungry when you got in. They're wrapped in foil on the counter, probably still warm."

Riley looked around the sparkling kitchen. Millie had left no evidence of her culinary endeavors but the food to be enjoyed. "Thank you, but you really didn't have to do all of this."

"Nonsense. We've got to get home, so I'll leave you in your grandfather's good hands." Millie's face brightened when she mentioned Grandpa.

Zane entered the kitchen just then, and he and Millie exchanged farewells.

Grandpa escorted Millie to her car then returned to the kitchen. "Thought you'd never get here, but now that you are, I'm exhausted. You wouldn't think me rude if I went to bed, would you?"

"Grandpa, this is your house. Don't be ridiculous." Riley pecked him on the cheek.

"Night, all." He disappeared up the stairs.

Zane slung his soft leather briefcase onto the table and began pulling out his laptop. A manila folder slid out onto the floor.

Riley leaned over to retrieve the file. A picture fell out. She picked it up and examined it. A woman who resembled Riley was wearing a locket and holding a cell phone to her ear. "This is the picture you told me about. I've seen this before."

Zane plugged in the computer and booted it. "Probably saw it in a magazine: That's where it came from. For some reason, John created a photo-quality picture from the magazine image to grab my attention in all of this." He frowned.

After attaching the card reader to the USB port, Zane placed the memory card inside and waited for the data to display. He groaned and thrust his head into his hands, grabbing hair with his fingers.

"What is it?"

"We need the key. Why can't I figure this out? It shouldn't be this complicated."

"Maybe I can help. But honestly, I don't understand how it all works. Maybe if you could explain it to me, it would remind me of something important that John said to me. Why don't you tell me exactly what you mean when you say 'key,' for starters?"

"As you know, John was working to build a new standard for encryption. All that means is changing data into a secret code through a mathematical algorithm—one that no one could get into. The problem is that no one *can* get into it." He released a nervous, frustrated laugh. "The only way to read it is to have the key. John's key is a short program, an algorithm like the encryption code itself."

"Then let's go over what we have."

"Nothing. We have nothing." Zane slid away from the table and moved to the counter. He stretched out his arms and pressed his hands against the edge, supporting his body.

Riley persisted. "There has to be something you've overlooked or you're not telling me. We have the disk, and we found the locket—only it was used to give us the disk." Riley closed her eyes and took in a deep breath. "And we have that picture, the first clue."

The picture. A memory flashed across her mind, and she grappled with it, trying to capture the thought. "The picture. There's more to the picture." She took it out of the folder again. "She looks like me, she's wearing a locket. . .and she is talking on a cell phone."

Adrenaline rushed through her. "Zane, I know where I've seen that picture before."

Zane turned to face her. "In a magazine—I told you already."

"No, it's on my camera phone."

His eyes widened. "Give it to me."

Riley pulled the cell from her purse. "He sent me the phone a couple of weeks before he died. I had mentioned I'd like to have a camera phone. I confess I've never learned how to use it to take pictures."

"I need the connections that came with this. Do you still have them?"

Riley retrieved the accessories from her room. "What does it all mean? What's so important about the picture?"

He spoke as he connected the phone to the laptop. "If I'm right, the key is in the picture. If John embedded a data stream into this digital picture on your phone, all I have to do is download the picture, and when I open it on the laptop, the code should self-extract. It would then act similar to a virus. In this case, the virus is an algorithm used to open the data."

Riley exhaled, amazed that she'd carried the key with her the entire time.

nineteen

Riley leaned over Zane's shoulder to watch as file names appeared on the monitor. It was difficult to comprehend that John had stored the only key on her phone to open whatever valuable secrets were contained on the disk, and she'd unknowingly kept it for him.

This near to Zane, she felt herself breathe in the scent of his cologne. A sudden, unpleasant thought confronted her. Once he finished solving the puzzle, he would be finished with Sanderford Farms because he'd found the key. It had been at the farm, with Riley, the entire time. The fact that she would no longer see him every day, if at all, disturbed her. She believed he would want to spend time with Chad, but it wouldn't be the same.

Riley put her hand over her heart and took a step back from where Zane sat staring at the computer screen. He struggled with his relationship with God. She knew that, yet she'd allowed herself to fall in love with him. She'd been so caught up in the suspense of solving John's mystery that she wasn't sure when it had happened.

"No." The word escaped without her permission. Though she'd thought it was inaudible, Zane glanced back at her.

"No, what? This is exactly what we wanted. This is it. It worked, Riley."

Zane slid away from the computer and stood. "Come here." He pulled her into his arms and held her. "I couldn't have done this without you. You know that, right?"

Though her emotions were in conflict with her judgment, Riley allowed herself to savor his embrace. "That's only because John sent me the key. He could just as easily have put it into your phone."

"True enough. But he wanted the key to be far away from here. And maybe he knew we'd be good for each other." He squeezed her.

A thrill rushed through Riley, and she wondered if Zane felt the same way about her that she did about him. A small comment window appeared in the center of the monitor. Zane had his back to it, so he couldn't see.

Riley freed herself from his embrace. "I think it's finished."

Zane sat in the chair to face the laptop again. He scrolled down the list of file names; then he selected and opened one of them. Riley wasn't certain why he'd singled it out. Copies of e-mails were pasted into a document along with other information.

"What does it all mean?" she asked.

"I'm not exactly sure, but it doesn't look good."

A twinge of panic rippled across her skin.

"It appears to be incriminating information linked to a government official." Zane rubbed his chin. "I don't want to read anything more, nor do I want to hold on to this. It needs to be turned over to the authorities."

"So you think that they used John to hack into the system to retrieve this information?"

"That's exactly what I think. They could have threatened his life or his family. I'm not sure. But he did the work. I believe he gave us the clues to ensure his life once he was finished. If something happened to him, then the criminals would be exposed, though they had no way of knowing how. That's where I'm confused, because it didn't work, and because of his death, we now hold volatile information in our hands."

Zane shut down the computer then snapped it closed. Frowning, he stood and looked at Riley. She knew her expression mirrored his.

"John's plan backfired, and he was killed." She wasn't certain she believed that aspect of Zane's theory. Still, the authorities would have to iron out all that had happened and why. "What if, and this is a big 'if,' John's death really was an accident?" Her mind began to wrap around the idea. "What if the bad guys, whoever they are, didn't kill him? He just simply died before they got what they wanted?"

ða

Zane walked down the corridor of Cyphorensic Technologies to make sure the entire premises had been vacated. Though his lease did not expire for another two months, he'd sold the office furniture. There was no reason for him to remain. After all that had transpired over the last several months, Zane could not bring himself to go forward with his company when it had played a role in John's predicament.

His partner and friend had made sure that Zane had the encryption software he'd created. It was on the disk. Though it was only in the alpha phase, Zane was able to sell the code. He put the money into a trust fund for Chad.

Even with all the information that Zane had supplied the investigators, no other conclusion could be reached but that John had been killed in an accident, not murdered, before he had been able to deliver the decryption code to the criminals. Eric's clients. They'd had a need, and he'd supplied the name—John's name. Eric had no knowledge of their dealings with John until they pressured him to help obtain the key. After the police questioned Eric, two men were arrested in connection with attempting to gain unauthorized access into a government computer system.

Zane hoped that Riley found consolation in the fact that John did not seem to have participated in the hacking job by choice. But he was threatened, and in the end, it appeared that he'd had no intention of delivering.

Zane stood in the center of the reception area and turned slowly. His gaze rested on the spot where Chelsea's desk had been. He hoped she loved her new job.

"I'll pray for you." He reflected on her words then whispered, "Thank you, Chelsea."

His heart told him that her prayers had been answered. After the tragedy with his brother and his parents' divorce, he thought that God didn't care about the details of his life. Didn't care about him. So Zane wanted no part of God. His life, to this point, had been built on creating an empire for himself. But it meant nothing.

As he looked at the vacated offices of his venture, the cold, stark truth wrapped around him. He could do anything he wanted, including start a new company, but nothing he did would matter without a relationship with God and His Son.

He reflected on the last few months spent at Sanderford Cranberry Farms. Without a doubt, he knew that God did care about him. He could see it all around him, as well as through the subtle ways God had whispered to his heart.

Zane bowed his head, and in his heart, he humbled himself before the Creator, asking for forgiveness and a new start. Once peace settled over him, assuring him that God had answered, he said good-bye to his company. Zane walked out the door, trusting in God to direct him to his next endeavor.

He turned to lock the plate glass double doors but instead pressed his forehead against one of them. The pain of regret burned in his stomach. He'd never been in the position he was in now—unsure of what he would do next. Learning to trust in God's direction would be a new experience.

Images of Riley and Chad would not let go of him. With a business failure fresh in his mind and on his résumé, he had nothing to offer the woman he loved. He smiled to himself. It was the first time he'd admitted that he loved her.

As Zane pulled the key out of the lock, footfalls interrupted his thoughts, and he turned away from the company doors. Riley approached with Chad in her arms. Zane's heart soared at the sight of her. She released Chad, and the boy ran to Zane, who lifted him with zeal and kissed him on the forehead.

Riley smiled at Zane. He couldn't remember if she'd ever been so beautiful.

"I didn't want you to have to face closing your company doors alone. Sorry we weren't here sooner."

A gust of wind whipped curls across her face. Zane swept the tendrils away from her green eyes, bringing a blush to her cheeks.

"I'm not sure if this is the right time for me to discuss this with you." She blew out a breath. "Grandpa agrees with me. We'd like you to be a partner in Sanderford Cranberry Farms. Permanently. He loves your business plan, your ideas of how to grow the farm to include processing and distribution, and frankly, so do I. It doesn't mean you can't still work in the software industry—"

Zane covered her lips with his fingers then leaned down to kiss her. Chad forced him to end the kiss all too soon. "I thought I knew what would make me happy. But I didn't— that is, until I met you. I can't think of anything I'd rather do than see you at the cranberry farm every day."

In his heart, he thanked God for sending the answer

already. He knew the gentle nudge he felt about Riley was God's urging, as well. "But first, I have a question for you, and I'm not sure what your grandfather will think about this."

Riley knitted her brows, and her smile flattened. "What is it?"

"I'm in love with you, Riley."

Moisture brimmed in her eyes, magnifying the love he saw in them. "Oh, Zane." She pressed her lips together and averted her gaze.

Pain ripped through his heart. "I'm sorry if I spoke too soon."

"No, it's just that I don't know where you stand with God."

His spirit soared. "I can settle that for you. I've resolved my issues and allowed Him back into my life." His smile beamed from within.

"Really?" Her face brightened.

"Really."

"I can see it written all over your face. You couldn't have made me happier. I love you, too." She melted into his embrace.

"Are you sure I can't make you happier? Because I haven't asked you the question yet."

Riley pushed away from him to look into his eyes. Her mouth dropped open.

"Riley O'Hare, will you marry me?"

She pressed both hands against her heart, tears streaming. "Yes, Zane Baldwyn, I will marry you!"

"Yes, Zshane Balwin, I merwy you." Chad grinned, revealing a mouth full of perfect white baby teeth.

epilogue

Riley stood in the foyer of the two-hundred-year-old church, waiting for the stained oak sanctuary doors to open; then she would glide up the red-carpeted aisle, stepping in cadence to the wedding march. They had planned for a small, quiet wedding.

She'd waited months for this spring day—the season when everything began anew. Both she and Zane needed to put their ordeal behind them and have an opportunity to focus on each other, free from the backdrop of the suspense that had shadowed their relationship. Though she still missed her brother and his wife and regretted the time she'd lost with them, Riley began to accept the loss—especially since she knew that they were with the Lord.

She had settled comfortably into her new role as a mother, and Chad's demeanor reflected his content. Though he'd lost both of his parents, all that mattered now was that he was loved and cherished. Zane would make a great father, and in fact, he was already fulfilling that role with Chad. She couldn't wait until they would officially become a family.

Her grandfather had agreed to allow Zane to build a new farmhouse on the property for the Baldwyn family. Riley inhaled deeply and widened her eyes to stem the tide of tears. She didn't want to cry on this day, but she knew she'd end up losing the battle.

"You look beautiful, Riley!" Her father's voice broke through her thoughts. Tall and stately, he paced across the wood flooring in his black tuxedo. He would walk her down the aisle to give her away. It thrilled her to see him again. With him living in California and her in Massachusetts, she wouldn't see him often. He stood teary-eyed, and she hoped he'd shed the tears for the both of them.

"Thank you. You know, in moving here, nothing turned out the way I planned, but at least I met Zane." Riley closed her eyes and inhaled deeply to calm her nerves.

Her sweaty palms made it difficult to grip the crimson-accented bouquet. She twisted the large ruby engagement ring on her finger. She smiled as she remembered when Zane had taken her for a walk among the oaks and maples beyond the cranberry beds. They'd shared a kiss under the trees; then he'd pulled the ring from his pocket. He'd presented her with the gem, explaining that it represented the bog rubies to remind them of how they fell in love.

Amazed, she could do nothing but love him and be grateful to God for bringing him into her life. It seemed that when she had embarked on a search for peace the storms had grown much fiercer. But they lasted only for a time.

Soon the growing season would begin all over again. Her life had changed as quickly as the seasons. As if on cue, the organ chords vibrated through the old structure, pulling her from her reverie, and the doors swung open. Zane stood at the end of the walkway.

Riley's heart pounded, reaching into her throat. She longed to be with him and wanted to hasten through, but the wedding ceremony would not be rushed any more than the cranberries would be hurried to ripen on the vine. As she took her first step down the aisle toward her future husband, she trembled. Her father gently squeezed her arm hooked through his and patted her hand, reassuring her.

She kept her focus on Zane, though she could still see the heads turning to watch her. Some gasped, and others softly remarked what a beautiful bride she made.

Her father spoke in his turn, giving her away. She stepped forward, and Zane took her hand. The pastor began to speak, and in her heart, she believed and agreed to every word. But she hardly heard them as her love spilled over for the handsome man standing next to her.

Once they were announced as man and wife, Zane and Riley shared a gentle kiss that signified the beginning. There was a season for everything, and now Riley would begin a new season of life, one she would spend with the man she loved.

A Letter To Our Readers

Dear Reader:
In order that we might better contribute to your reading enjoyment, we would appreciate your taking a few minutes to respond to the following questions. We welcome your comments and read each form and letter we receive. When completed, please return to the following:

Fiction Editor
Heartsong Presents
PO Box 719
Uhrichsville, Ohio 44683

1. Did you enjoy reading *Seasons of Love* by Elizabeth Goddard?
   ❑ Very much! I would like to see more books by this author!
   ❑ Moderately. I would have enjoyed it more if

   _____

   _____

   _____

2. Are you a member of **Heartsong Presents**? ❑ Yes ❑ No
   If no, where did you purchase this book? _____

   _____

3. How would you rate, on a scale from 1 (poor) to 5 (superior), the cover design? _____

4. On a scale from 1 (poor) to 10 (superior), please rate the following elements.

   ____ Heroine   ____ Plot
   ____ Hero   ____ Inspirational theme
   ____ Setting   ____ Secondary characters

5. These characters were special because? _____

_____

_____

6. How has this book inspired your life? _____

_____

_____

7. What settings would you like to see covered in future
   Heartsong Presents books? _____

_____

_____

8. What are some inspirational themes you would like to see
   treated in future books? _____

_____

_____

9. Would you be interested in reading other **Heartsong
   Presents** titles? ❏ Yes ❏ No

10. Please check your age range:
   ❏ Under 18   ❏ 18-24
   ❏ 25-34   ❏ 35-45
   ❏ 46-55   ❏ Over 55

Name_____

Occupation _____

Address _____

City, State, Zip_____

KANSAS WEDDINGS

3 stories in 1

Three Kansas women have difficult decisions to make and burdens to bear. Will these women find love despite their handships?

Contemporary, paperback, 352 pages, 5³/₁₆" x 8"

Hearts♥ng

Any 12
Heartsong
Presents titles
for only
$27.00*

CONTEMPORARY ROMANCE IS CHEAPER BY THE DOZEN!

Buy any assortment of twelve *Heartsong Presents* titles and save 25% off the already discounted price of $2.97 each!

*plus $3.00 shipping and handling per order and sales tax where applicable.
If outside the U.S. please call 740-922-7280 for shipping charges.

HEARTSONG PRESENTS TITLES AVAILABLE NOW:

(If ordering from this page, please remember to include it with the order form.)

Presents